I0726372

STRIKEFORCE AGENT
VALERIE INGLEWOOD

BAD BLOOD

T.K. WILDE

Dreamstone Publishing © 2016

www.dreamstonepublishing.com

ISBN: 1925499278

ISBN-13:   978-1-925499-27-8

Disclaimer

This is a work of fiction. Any resemblance to persons living or deceased is purely coincidental, and is not intended.

Dedication

To my readers – without you, there would be no stories.

To all of my family and friends, who support me when I am writing, and make it possible for books to get finished – thank you!

Table of Contents

Chapter 1

Machine gun fire spattered the side of the building and shattered the bricks. A handful of bullets crashed through the plate glass window. Shards of broken glass rained down on Valerie's head. She kept her eyes closed until the tinkling stopped and the gunfire moved away around the corner.

Valerie raised her head and looked around. Plates of food sat overturned on the floor, and broken plates and soggy napkins littered the place. A few minutes before, Valerie had been sitting down to a hearty breakfast with her partner, Charlene Brockworth, to celebrate the newest member of the Strikeforce Team.

Jeff Everson had earned his place, with a special commendation from Colonel Tomlinson, and now he and his partner, Tiko Bennetta, were assigned to work with Valerie and Charlene on the Denver mob war.

But their celebratory breakfast had just come to an abrupt halt, as gunfire tore the cafe apart, and everyone in the place scattered for cover. Valerie aimed her service pistol at the empty hole where the front window used to be, but the shooter was long gone.

Charlene's voice rang through the remains of the cafe. "Are you all right, Valerie?"

"I'm fine," Valerie replied. "Are you okay?"

A crash answered her. Charlene stepped out of the shadows with her pistol in her hand. "I've had enough of this gangland stuff. Let's go back to the Mackenzie Lodge. At least it was quiet there."

"It was quiet at EdenCloud, too, and I wouldn't want to go back there. Give me the city any day of the week." Valerie brushed broken glass off her clothes and holstered her weapon. "Did you see anything? Did you get a look at anyone in the car?"

Charlene shook her head.

"No one ever sees anything in drive-bys like this. Even if we'd got a look at the shooters, they would probably have been wearing masks."

A few customers poked their heads out of their hiding places. "Where are the others?"

Before Charlene could answer, another explosion of gunfire broke the stillness. Valerie and Charlene hit the floor, but this time, the spray didn't end and fade away. It grew louder and more menacing. Valerie crawled under the nearest table and drew her weapon again.

A moment later, a pair of legs kicked the door open. Valerie caught sight of a man's figure, cradling a machine gun in his hands, but she couldn't see his face. He leveled his gun and let loose another deadly barrage of bullets. They splintered the wooden table over Valerie's head, and she scuttled for cover.

The only place she could find to hide was the waiter's station, and she crawled behind it.

The heavy plywood counter protected her from the bullets, but she couldn't see anything back there. She took one peek around the corner and saw the strange legs walking in her direction.

All of a sudden, a hand closed around her arm. She nearly jumped out of her skin, but, when she turned to look behind her, she found herself nose to nose with Jeff Everson. "Valerie! I've been looking everywhere for you." Jeff whispered against her ear.

"What are you doing back here, Jeff?" she asked, also whispering.

"The same thing you're doing here," he replied. "I'm saving my bacon. I don't care if I'm a federal agent now. I'm not going out there to face a man with a machine gun when I've only got a .44 to defend myself with."

Valerie snickered. "Don't worry. We're all doing the same thing. Nobody wants to lose their life playing the hero. It wouldn't do any good anyway." The machine gun farted again, and Jeff and Valerie huddled close behind the counter. "What the devil is going on out there? He's already destroyed the place. Why doesn't he leave?"

Bullets rattling against the walls interrupted their conversation. In the din of splintering sheetrock and crashing crockery, Jeff leaned over and kissed her. Valerie pulled back in surprise. "What was that for?"

He grinned.

"Just saying hello. We haven't had a moment together since I joined the Strikeforce Team."

He tried to kiss her again, but she shoved him back. "What are you trying to do? We're in the middle of a shoot-out."

"What better time?" he asked. "No one will see us. Your partner is across the room and...." He glanced around. "I don't see my partner anywhere. No one will know."

He kissed her, and the fire of desire blocked out everything else. Valerie let her mouth fall open, and his sweet saliva prickled her tongue. When would they find a moment to go off alone together? He would move into the Strikeforce penthouse any day now. What would happen to their relationship then?

The bullets stopped flying, and the silence brought Valerie back to the present. She pushed him away again, but without much conviction. "We'd better not. We're supposed to be on the job."

He moved away, but his eyes didn't leave her face. "Just remember I'm coming for you."

"I can't wait." Valerie cocked her ears at the sound of footsteps crunching through the broken glass. They came close to the waiters' station, but then they passed on. The shooter sure was taking his time about destroying the place. Wasn't he worried about someone recognizing him?

She glanced over at Jeff. To her horror, he rose up on his knees and peeked over the counter at the shooter. The man turned, and sprayed the back wall with bullets. Jeff dropped down to the floor next to her again. Valerie grabbed his arm.

"What do you think you're doing? Are you trying to get your head shot off?"

"I had to see who it was," he replied. "If there was any chance of identifying him, I had to take the chance."

Valerie hauled him down to the floor. "Don't you ever try anything like that again."

"Don't worry," he replied. "I didn't get shot."

"So did you get a look at him?" she asked.

Jeff shook his head. "Charlene was right. He's wearing a mask."

Another volley of bullets broke off their conversation, but when the cafe fell silent again, a sinking feeling told Valerie the attack was over. The shooter's footsteps crunched through the glass on his way back toward the door. Then he disappeared outside.

No one moved a muscle or made a peep. Charlene didn't call out again or stand up. Valerie and Jeff stayed behind the counter for what seemed like a long time. In the end, Jeff got up on his hands and knees. "It's safe now. He's gone."

They got to their feet. Charlene emerged from a pile of overturned tables on the other side of the café, surveyed the room and stuck her pistol into the holster at her back. She met Valerie and Jeff at the waiters' station. "Well, this place is a write-off. I hope their insurance is up to date."

"I don't think most business insurance policies cover shoot-'em-ups," Jeff remarked.

Valerie put her weapon away. "They can list it under 'Acts of God'."

"This was no act of God." Charlene took out her phone. "Good morning, Colonel Tomlinson. Yes, Sir. That's why I'm calling. We just had another shoot-out here at the Morning Maven Cafe. Yep. Will do." She hung up. "He's assigning us to investigate. I thought he might. Where's Tiko?"

Tiko Bennetta stuck his head with his slicked-back hair out from behind the kitchen door. "I'm in here. We got a situation."

"What's going on?" Charlene asked.

"This wasn't your typical gangland shoot-out," Tiko replied. "This was a premeditated murder. Come have a look."

They followed him through the kitchen to the back office, where the manager sat at his desk with the ballpoint pen hanging from his fingers. His head hung down onto his chest and his mouth dropped open. No one would ever have guessed he hadn't fallen asleep at his desk. Only the black stain spreading over the back of his shirt gave mute testimony that he wouldn't wake up again.

Tiko pointed to the torn cloth of the victim's T-shirt. "Four bullets to the back and they weren't machine gun bullets, either. That shoot-up out front was just a distraction. The killer must have snuck in through the back door, shot Tony, and then beat it while the rest of us were cowering in fear."

Charlene got on her phone again. "Hey, Mort. It's Charlene Brockworth here. Yeah, we've got a stiff for you at 275 Ironwood Street. The Morning Maven Cafe, in the manager's office. Great. See you then." She hung up again. "The Crime Lab is on the way."

Valerie bent over the manager. "What do you know about the vic, Tiko?"

"Tony?" Tiko asked. "Everybody knows Tony Eno. He's a legend in this town."

"Then how come I never heard of him?" Charlene asked.

"Because you're not Italian," Tiko replied.

"Neither are you," Charlene shot back. "Now stop playing games and tell us what you know about him. I guess he was more than just the manager of a coffee shop, or the gangsters wouldn't have made such an effort to kill him."

"You're right, he was a lot more than a manager," Tiko replied. "He was the son of Edith Skipperingham. That's how he got this position in the first place."

"Edith Skipperingham?" Charlene exclaimed. "But she's Frank Lukeman's wife."

"*Ex*-wife," Tiko corrected her. "They split up, and she got bigger than he ever was. It looks like she took half his money and set herself up in business to compete with him. They've been at each other's throats ever since."

"If that's true," Valerie pointed out, "then this Tony Eno would be Frank's son, too. He wouldn't kill his own son to get back at Edith."

Tiko shook his head, but his black eyes twinkled. "Wrong again, Virginia. Tony is Edith's son by another man. Some people say she cheated on Frank and got pregnant while they were still married. Other people think she got pregnant before she got together with Frank. Either way, one thing is certain."

"Enlighten us, O Master," Charlene said, grinning at Tiko.

Tiko puffed himself up. "His father is Danny Seagall."

A hush fell over the group. Jeff looked around. "Did I miss something?"

Valerie sighed. "You just started with the Strikeforce Team, so you don't know. If you'd been around Denver very long, you would know that Danny Seagall is Frank Lukeman's worst enemy. They've been warring for twenty years."

Tiko interrupted. "And now you know why."

"So Frank Lukeman killed Danny and Edith's son," Jeff replied. "That makes the case pretty straightforward."

"Not exactly," Valerie replied. "Frank might have ordered this hit, but he wouldn't pull the trigger himself. He would have sent one of his boys to do the job. Anyway, it's our job to collect the evidence and prove that he did order the hit. It could have been someone else."

"Like who?" Tiko asked. "Tony had a thousand friends and no enemies that I know of. If Frank didn't kill him, I don't know who did."

At that moment, a woman's scream ripped through the cafe. The four investigators went back out to the waiters' station. A man with sweat streaming down his face met them at the door. He grabbed Charlene's hand and pulled her across the room. "He's over here. Quick! You have to call the police. You can still save him."

They followed him across the room. Behind a cluster of overturned tables, a woman knelt by another man, who was lying still and stiff on the floor.

The first thing Valerie noticed was his suit. He wore an immaculate, pinstriped Armani suit and polished leather brogues. Who dressed like that to come down to their corner coffee shop for breakfast?

Blood stained the dead man's crisp white shirt, and bullet holes marred his jacket. The woman pressed his hand to her heart and sobbed. The first man tugged at Charlene's hand. "Quick! Call the police!"

Charlene sighed. "We are the police. Whoever did this, we're the ones who will investigate."

"But you can save him," the man insisted. "Call the paramedics. They can hook him up to their machines and save him."

Charlene gazed down at the motionless form. In front of their eyes, a pool of blood spread out on the floor under the victim's back. "I'm afraid no one can save him now. The Crime Lab will be here soon, and after that, the Coroner will take your friend's body."

"He's not my friend," the man told her. "He's my brother."

Charlene's head came up in a hurry. "Your brother?"

The man nodded. "He came into town for business and we met here for breakfast. We don't go out very often, but we decided to make this a special occasion. Then *this* had to happen."

"Look, Mister.... What did you say your name was?" Charlene asked.

"I'm Tom Duvall, and this is my wife Margaret," he replied. "My brother was Tim Duvall."

"I'm very sorry for your loss, Mr. Duvall," Charlene replied, "but your brother is the unfortunate victim of some very nasty mob activity that's been plaguing the area for some time. We've been trying to break it up, and this was just another battle in a very long war. I'm afraid your brother got caught in the crossfire."

Tom looked around the battered cafe in desperation. "But that's impossible. This is Denver, the Mile-High City. There's no mob activity here. I've lived here for forty years, and nothing like this ever happened before."

Charlene's shoulders sagged.

"I know it's hard to believe, but the mob elements in this war have kept their activities under cover for a long time. They only started breaking out onto the streets about a year ago. That's when we got called in."

Tom stared down at his brother.

"This can't be happening."

"I'm so sorry." Charlene waved toward the door. "Let's get you two out of here. You'll feel better in the open air."

Tom shook his head. "I can't leave him."

Valerie studied the dead man. He didn't come to Denver to transact business in a suit like that – not any legal kind of business, anyway. Charlene escorted Tom out of the cafe, but Valerie couldn't tear herself away from this second victim. Jeff appeared at her side.

"The Crime Lab is here. We have to go."

Valerie nodded and bent over Margaret. She still bathed the victim's pale hand with her tears.

"Come on, Mrs. Duvall. We have to leave now to let the Crime Lab people work."

They met Tom and Charlene on the street outside, just as the Crime Lab techs pulled up in their unmarked white van.

"There's one victim in the front under the tables and another one in the manager's office."

Tom looked around, but it was obvious that he didn't see anything in front of him. Margaret wept silent tears and held Valerie's hand in a death grip. Valerie nodded toward Charlene's car a few parking spaces away. "We'd better take them home. They can't go alone."

Charlene nodded and they steered the bereaved couple towards the car. Valerie glanced over her shoulder and spotted Jeff staring at her. At the same moment, Tiko came out of the cafe and said something to Jeff. He waved his arms, and his cheeks flushed with excitement. Jeff turned away, and the two men crossed the street to their own car.

Where were they going? When would Valerie see Jeff again? He'd been too busy with his initiation procedures and assignments to spend much time in the office. And Valerie was busy with the organized crime training she needed to complete before Colonel Tomlinson would assign her to the Denver mob war.

Of course, Charlene had kept their observation of Jeff's try-out for the Strikeforce Team a secret.

He never knew that Valerie was watching him on the rifle range and the obstacle course. And she'd never been near enough to tell him – until just now behind the cafe counter, with bullets flying. Leave it to him to take that opportunity to kiss her.

Chapter 2

Charlene dropped into her chair behind her desk, and Valerie kicked off her shoes and settled on the couch with her computer in front of her. "What do you make of it, Valerie?"

Valerie shrugged. "I'm surprised our shooter didn't kill more people in the cafe. You could almost start to believe he aimed for Tim Duvall's Armani suit."

Charlene chuckled. "So you noticed that, too, huh? I wondered if you did. Not exactly the uniform of your average traveling businessman, is it?"

"What about Margaret?" Valerie replied. "She was awfully sad about a brother-in-law she'd only just met. I'd say there's more to the happy family than meets the eye."

Jeff swiveled his chair around. "Here's what I don't understand. So Frank Lukeman wanted Tony Eno dead. He sure went to a lot of trouble to do it. Why did he have to shoot up the whole cafe and kill innocent bystanders in the process? He could have snuck in the back door after closing time, when he knew Tony would be alone, and shot him in the back. End of story. We probably never would have known it was a mob hit."

Tiko set his coffee cup down on his desk.

"Maybe he wanted us, and everyone else, to know he did it. Maybe he wanted to stick it in Edith's face that he'd killed her son."

Charlene shook her head. "That is so seriously twisted, Tiko. I swear you missed your calling in life. You should have been a mobster."

He grinned at her. "I was one before I joined Strikeforce. I worked for Carlos Pena down in Santiago for ten years before I went straight. Thinking like a mobster is second nature to me."

Jeff examined his partner with a critical eye.

"Then maybe you can tell us how the shooter managed to hit the one guy in the whole cafe who was sitting behind a potted plant, behind a wall, and around a corner. From what I remember, bullets were flying everywhere. The four of us were right in his line of fire. If anyone was going to get hit, it should have been one of us."

"We've been trained to hit the deck when the shooting starts," Charlene pointed out.

Jeff shook his head. "Everybody in the cafe hit the deck at the same time. The guy walked right past us, and he aimed his fire above the other customers."

Charlene leaned forward in her chair.

"Are you saying that you saw more than Tiko and I did? Are you saying that you saw more than seasoned federal agents? You're getting a little bit too big for your boots there, aren't you, sonny?"

Jeff shrugged. "I'm just saying what I saw."

"What exactly are you saying?" Valerie asked him.

"I'm saying the shooter when out of his way to hit Tim Duvall," Jeff replied. "He deliberately left the four of us alive, and if he was a mob hit man, he must have known exactly who we were. He also deliberately left Tom and Margaret Duvall alive, even though they were hiding under the same table and were crouched right next to Tim."

Charlene shook her head but didn't say anything. Tiko chuckled under his breath.

"What about Tony?" Valerie asked. "If the shooter went after Tim, how do you explain Tony winding up dead at the same time? The shooter didn't kill him."

Jeff shook his head.

"We assumed, when we saw Tony, that the shooter destroyed the cafe to distract everybody from the real murder going on. Then, when we found Tim, we assumed he'd been hit by accident, by stray fire. But we could be wrong about both of those things. The two murders could be related."

Charlene threw up her hands with a bellow of annoyance and leapt out of her chair.

"I'm not listening to any more of this. You're crazy, dude. You just started on the Strikeforce Team, and you're letting your investigative power rush to your head. Tim Duvall *was* hit by stray fire. That's all. He was a stranger in Denver. He had no connection to Frank Lukeman, or Danny Seagall, or anybody else we're investigating. Now sit back and let the experts do their jobs."

Tiko held up a hand.

"No, wait a minute. I think he might be onto something. I want to hear what he has to say. Go ahead, man. Give us the whole story, chapter, and verse."

Jeff got up and started pacing back and forth between the desks. He waved his arms to punctuate his comments. Valerie gazed up at him and drank in every word.

"Let's say our friend Tim wasn't some schmo businessman who just happened to visit his brother while he was in town. He certainly didn't dress like one, and I challenge you to show me the traveling businessman who can afford the kind of shoes he was wearing."

Tiko nodded.

"Keep going, homeboy. I'm right there with you."

Jeff started talking faster.

"Let's say he was here for something else – or that his so-called business was related to one of our mob characters. Let's say, just for kicks, that he worked for Danny Seagall. Or maybe he worked for Frank Lukeman, and Frank wanted to get rid of him. Either way, Frank had two targets at the Morning Maven, and he decided to hit them both at once."

Charlene threw up her hands again and turned away.

"You're crazy. That's what you are. You're stone cold crazy. You've watched *The Godfather* too many times, and you're inventing stories out of your imagination."

Jeff stopped pacing and turned to face her.

"You can't tell me that Tim Duvall wasn't a target. He even dressed like a gangster – a high-end gangster with a heck of a lot of money in the bank. We already know that Frank had a motive to kill Tony. Why wouldn't he plan to kill two birds with one stone?"

Tiko nodded again.

"I'm willing to go along with this for the sake of a working hypothesis. Let's say Frank wanted to execute two hits in one. He hired the shooter to blast the ever-lovin' bejeezus out of the cafe. He knew we were there, so he wanted to get us down on the floor where we couldn't stop him."

"And don't forget we couldn't see anything when we were on the floor, either," Jeff pointed out.

Tiko nodded. "Right. So there we were, lying on our faces with our butts pointed up in the air. The shooter kills Tim and some other mystery killer walks in the back door and kills Tony."

Jeff hesitated. He stopped in mid-stride and dropped his eyes to the ground.

"It doesn't sound very likely when you put it that way."

Charlene whirled around. "That's what I'm talking about."

Valerie gazed up at Jeff's face. The blood colored his cheeks, and excitement lit up his eyes. Where did he come up with that theory? She couldn't have come up with that theory as fast as he did. Not even Tiko and Charlene could fire off a cock-eyed theory like that when they'd just walked in the door from some mob shooting. None of them had the guts to open their mouths about something as wild as that.

And yet, how could he be wrong? Every detail of his theory fit the evidence. His mind put together the puzzle pieces faster than all three of them combined, and he'd only just started on the team. What kind of whirlwind had landed in their laps? What would Colonel Tomlinson say when he found out? Then again, maybe Colonel Tomlinson already knew. Maybe that's why he'd selected Jeff for the team in the first place.

"I agree with Jeff," Valerie murmured. "As crazy as it sounds, this theory is the only possible scenario that fits the evidence. It's the only one that makes any kind of sense."

Tiko clapped his hands.

"That's what I'm talking about. That's my man."

Charlene smacked her lips and spun away on her heel.

"This is mutiny! You two are supposed to be in training, not telling seasoned veterans their jobs. You're supposed to sit back and listen while we solve the murders."

"When did I ever sit back and listen?" Valerie asked. "I solved the murders from our very first case together. You would be dead right now if I hadn't."

Charlene glared at her.

"Don't you start telling me what you did and didn't do. No one can tell me Frank Lukeman ordered a hit on Tim Duvall."

"Maybe he didn't order a hit on Tim," Valerie replied. "Maybe he ordered a hit on Tom and the shooter hit the wrong person. Did you ever think of that?"

"Maybe he ordered a hit on Margaret and the shooter hit the wrong person," Tiko added.

Jeff shook his head again.

"We're talking about a contract killer. He went there to kill Tim and that's who he killed. If he hit Tom or Margaret or anybody else by accident, he would have kept on shooting until he hit his target. He wouldn't have walked away and left his target still alive."

Tiko clapped his hands again and let out a hair-raising whoop.

"Will you listen to this guy? Listen to the way his mind works. That's my main man! That's my partner."

Valerie couldn't stop herself from grinning. At least Tiko had spoken up for Jeff. He'd spoken the words that were ringing through Valerie's own mind. What a brain that man had! Then she spotted Charlene fuming on the other side of her desk. She changed the subject.

"Let's get back to the question of Tony. We all agree that he was murdered in cold blood. If we can't agree on Tim, let's focus on what we know. Someone walked into Tony's office and shot him several times in the back."

Charlene glanced at her. Her expression didn't soften, but at least she was willing to listen.

"What did you have in mind?" Tiko asked.

Valerie swiveled her chair back to her computer.

"I just ran a search on Tony Eno. He had no restaurant experience at all. He never would have set foot in the Morning Maven if his mother hadn't used her influence to get him the job."

"That doesn't sound like much of a target for a mob hit," Jeff pointed out.

"He wasn't a mob hit," Tiko replied. "He was killed in revenge for his mother's infidelity."

Jeff held up both hands.

"Hold on there. Not so fast. We're jumping to way too many conclusions. First of all, we have no proof at all that Frank Lukeman ordered hits on anybody. We also don't have any proof whatsoever that Edith Skipperingham was unfaithful. She could have had Tony long before she ever met Frank."

Tiko's shoulders sagged.

"Oh. Right. I forgot about that."

Valerie studied her computer.

"The city records show Tony's date of birth as two years before Frank and Edith got married. But Tony's birth certificate lists his father as Frank Lukeman."

"If Frank is Tony's father, how did he get the name Eno?" Jeff asked. "You said his father was Danny Seagall."

"So he was two years old when Edith met Frank," Tiko pointed out.

"When Edith married Frank," Valerie corrected him. "They could have known each other and been involved long before they got married."

"If Tony was conceived through Edith's relationship with another man," Tiko asked, "Frank wouldn't want him to carry his own name, would he?"

"But you just said Frank is listed on the birth certificate as Tony's father," Jeff replied. "You can't tell me he didn't want Tony to have his name but didn't mind being named as his father. Either Frank didn't want to have anything to do with the kid, or he didn't care how he was conceived and wanted to be Tony's father regardless. You can't have it both ways."

"There's one more possibility," Valerie added. "It's possible Frank really is Tony's father, and all those tall tales of infidelity are just urban legend."

"If that's true," Charlene told her, "then we're dead in the water without a theory."

Chapter 3

Valerie stopped in front of the Strikeforce Team's penthouse suite, on the top floor of their office building, in downtown Denver. She glanced over her shoulder at Jeff.

"Did Tiko give you a key of your own?"

Jeff took a key out of his pocket. He unlocked the door and they entered the suite.

"Tiko said the Team would send my things up from the locker room."

Valerie snorted.

"That's what they always say. When they drag you out of bed at four in the morning and whisk you off to Europe or somewhere else, they say the Team will send your things along for you."

"Don't they?" Jeff asked.

"In my experience," Valerie replied, "you'll have your cases solved before your things leave the building. My advice to you is to always carry a toothbrush and toothpaste and a comb in your pocket, and maybe a clean pair of underwear. I've been caught more than once with nothing but the clothes on my back."

"Maybe you're just really good at solving cases," Jeff suggested.

"That's what Charlene says," Valerie replied. "But from what I saw from you in the office today, you'll be the same way. Remember the Boy Scout motto: *Be Prepared.*"

"Thanks for the advice." He closed the door behind them and surveyed the penthouse. "Where is everybody?"

"Most of them are on assignment," Valerie replied. "That's the way it is with the Team. We spend most of our time skipping around the planet from one case to another. We don't spend much time here except between cases, debriefing and catching up on training. Charlene and Tiko are meeting with Colonel Tomlinson about the murders at the cafe this morning. They'll be back later."

Jeff stuck his key chain back in his pocket and strolled through the suite.

"It's a pretty nice place."

"A lot better than the Mackenzie Lodge, don't you think?" she asked.

He nodded.

"I could get used to this, although I'm going to have to get used to sharing the place with other people. I haven't lived with anybody else in years."

"You have your own room with adjacent bathroom," Valerie told him. "Everybody has their own private suite. Come on. I'll show you."

She led him down a hall lined on either side with doors.

"This is my room."

She threw her bedroom door open, and he stuck his head inside. He noted the fresh white bed in the middle, the neat desk on the other side, and the bathroom door standing open. A pair of French doors looked out onto a balcony with a sweeping view of the Rocky Mountains in the distance.

"Nice view. Does everybody have a balcony?"

Valerie nodded and closed the door.

"This is yours down here. All the suites are laid out the same way."

She opened the door next to her own, and Jeff stepped into an empty room identical to Valerie's. It only lacked the pictures of her family and her dogs and her friends on the wall above her desk. Another set of French doors opened onto another balcony, and the mountains hung there outside these windows, too.

Jeff nodded. "This will do very nicely."

Valerie shifted from one foot to the other.

"You don't think it will get uncomfortable.... us working together, I mean? We'll be living right next door to each other, and now with you and Tiko and me and Charlene all assigned to this mob case together, we'll be together twenty-four hours a day."

"So what are you saying?" he asked. "What could get uncomfortable about that?"

"We might get sick of each other," she replied. "Or our relationship could turn sour, and we could start to hate each other. And then there's the possibility of Tiko and Charlene finding out about us. Charlene got really bent out of shape when we met at the lodge. If she finds out we're...." She trailed off.

A smile twitched at the corners of his mouth. His intense gaze made Valerie fidget.

"We're what?"

"You know," she blurted out.

"If she finds out there's anything going on between us, she'll hit the roof. I wouldn't want either of us to lose our place on the team because of our relationship."

He broke into a full-blown smile.

"Do we have a relationship?"

Valerie pursed her lips, looking annoyed.

"You kissed me this morning in the middle of a shoot-out, and we slept together twice at the lodge. Of course we have a relationship."

He took a step closer to her, and his presence sent an irresistible vibration through her being.

"We slept together a lot more than twice."

"You know what I mean," she muttered.

Jeff sighed.

"Look, Valerie. I tried out for the Strikeforce Team to be near you. I know your place on this team means everything to you, and I would never do anything to jeopardize it. If our relationship – or whatever you want to call it—starts to get in the way of our working together, we'll just back off and keep it strictly professional. I think we can both handle that, don't you?"

Valerie's eyes widened.

"Do you mean that?"

He put his hand on his chest.

"Scout's honor. Besides, you just said that most of the agents on the team are out of the area most of the time. You and Charlene won't be assigned to work with me and Tiko forever. We'll be working on different cases in different parts of the country, so we'll be out each other's hair."

Valerie broke into a radiant smile.

"You're right. I didn't think of that."

"Living next door to each other in this penthouse doesn't mean we're getting married," Jeff went on. "If kissing and fooling around is nice for both of us, why shouldn't we do it? If it isn't working for us, we'll stop. It's as simple as that."

"You make it sound like falling off a log," she told him.

He chuckled. "Not exactly."

Valerie started for the door.

"Would you like me to show you around the rest of the penthouse? That door at the end of the hall leads up to a garden on the roof."

He followed her to the door, but before she could pass through it, he caught her by the hand and pulled her back into the room.

"You can show me around later." He pushed the door closed, and it shut with a click.

Valerie's eyes widened, and her nostrils flared. Was he... would he.... He loomed over her with his dark eyes blazing. He knew what she wanted, and he wouldn't hold back. She knew him well enough to know that.

He folded her into his arms, and the delicious wine of his kiss flooded her brain. For a moment, it was as if the explosion of gunfire deafened her and sent her reeling. But that mind-blowing explosion was only the fireworks of her hunger for him, going off in her mind.

His hand cupped the back of her neck, and she relaxed into his grip. He could do what he wanted with her, and she would experience the same pleasure that she always did with him. She never questioned him when he held her in his arms, and all her doubts about the future dissolved into clouds of bliss.

He supported her weight in the crook of his arm. Her feet drifted off the floor. He carried her across the room and laid her down on the bed. His jacket vanished, and so did her shoes. He stretched out next to her, and their bodies tangled together on the clean, soft sheets.

Hours later, Valerie turned up her face to receive his kiss again, and this time, her eyes opened.

"I've been thinking."

"Uh-oh," he grinned. "I thought I smelled something burning."

Valerie gave him a playful smack on the arm. "I'm serious. Something's bothering me about the case."

"Don't you think you should be talking to Charlene about this?" he asked. "I'm the rookie on this team."

"You might be a rookie," she replied. "But you're already a top-notch investigator. You're the one who came up with the idea that the two murders could be connected, and I trust you to float my idea past you first."

He propped his head on his bent arm. "All right. Fire away. I'm all ears."

"You said that the shooter in the cafe was a contract killer who wouldn't stop until he hit his target," Valerie began.

"If he came from Frank Lukeman," Jeff replied, "he must have been. Frank wouldn't send an amateur to do a job like that."

"I just finished a six-week Federal training course on organized crime," Valerie went on. "Colonel Tomlinson wouldn't assign me to the Seagall-Lukeman war until I finished it."

Jeff nodded. "You told me that."

"Well, in this course, we learned a few things about contract assassinations," Valerie explained. "The assassins are meticulous about their weapons, their gear, even their clothes. Most of them have elaborate rituals they go through to get into the right mind frame before they go out to knock somebody off."

Jeff snorted.

"It sounds like the Olympics."

Valerie smiled.

"Something like that. Anyway, this course told us that they usually wear comfortable clothing that allows them to move freely. They'll wear sweat pants and a T-shirt, maybe some sneakers – clothes that will allow them to move quickly if they have to run for it."

Jeff frowned.

"I think I see where this is going."

"The course also told us that they'll sometimes wear heavy steel-toed boots if they're going into a dangerous area," Valerie went on. "They take every detail of the hit into account before they even walk through the door."

Jeff nodded. "Now give me the punch line."

Valerie took a deep breath.

"That shooter at the cafe was wearing a suit and patent leather shoes. If he planned to shoot up the cafe and then walk in to kill Tim Duvall, he would have been wearing stronger shoes to protect his feet from all that broken glass. He was even wearing a tie with a pearl tie tack. That was no contract killer."

Jeff let out his breath. "I see what you mean. But we've been operating under the assumption that this shoot-out was part of the larger mob war. If it wasn't, then who shot up the cafe?"

"I don't know," Valerie replied. "But I'm going to find out.

Chapter 4

"What have you got?" Jeff asked.

Valerie bent over her computer.

"Absolutely nothing. Tony Eno had no mob connections at all besides his mother, Edith. Most of these guys have at least been implicated in some crimes, if not done hard prison time for their organizations. Tony was as clean as a whistle."

"So was Edith," Tiko looked up from his computer. "Her only connection to the mob was her marriage to Frank Lukeman."

"What about all her moving and shaking in the business world?" Charlene asked. "The word on the street says she's had her fingers in a dozen pies all the way up to the Federal level."

Tiko shook his head and hit a few more keys on his laptop.

"All legit. After she left Frank, she started her own corporation and made gazillions in State and Federal contracts. She's got every politician in the Western US eating out of her hand, but she's always kept her nose clean. I guess she didn't want to have anything more to do with the criminal world after her time with Frank."

Jeff turned his back on his own computer.

"I can't find any connection between Tim Duvall and the mob, either. He wasn't working for Frank or Danny Seagall."

"Who did he work for?" Valerie asked.

"He worked for a little organic food distributor out of Salt Lake City," he replied. "It's called Green Harvest. It services mostly fundamentalist Christian types who want pure food untainted by the hand of man."

Charlene snorted.

"That sounds like EdenCloud."

"Nothing like that," Jeff replied. "This is the real deal. All their products have organic certification, and the business sells through an online outlet."

"So what did Tim do?" Valerie asked. "I thought he was a traveling salesman."

"Tom didn't say he was a traveling salesman," Jeff corrected her. "He said his brother came to Denver on business, and he visited his family while he was here. Tim's job title was Regional Manager. He could have been checking on their Denver area distribution center. He could have been researching the market in this area. We really don't know."

Charlene closed her laptop.

"We'll just have to find out. Valerie and I will go talk to the bereaved family again and see what we can find out."

"How are you going to do that without tipping them off?" Tiko asked.

"If you show up at their house asking questions, they might catch on that you think their brother's death wasn't an accident."

"If they have any clue, then they know a lot more about his activities than they're letting on," Charlene replied. "Come on, Valerie. Let's go."

"Hang on a minute." Valerie clicked her mouse. "There's another potential lead here."

"What's that?" Charlene asked.

"Tony had a girlfriend," Valerie replied. "A young lady by the name of....."

"Stephanie Bowen," Tiko interrupted.

Valerie's head shot up.

"Do you know about her?"

"Everybody knows about her," he replied. "She was glued to his hip. The two of them used to show up to the Swinging Sixties dance club downtown and set the place on fire. They were supposed to get married next summer, and the papers were buzzing with the news. Everybody knows about Tony and Stephanie."

Valerie shot out of her chair.

"Well, why didn't you tell us before? She could tell us who might have wanted to kill Tony."

"I thought we were looking at Frank Lukeman," Tiko shot back. "What happened to the jealous stepfather?"

"I don't see how he could be so jealous with his name on the victim's birth certificate," Jeff added. "Anyway, if Lukeman went to the trouble of hiring a hit man to bump off Tim Duvall, why wouldn't he use the same guy to bump off Tony? Why would he use two hit men?"

Charlene grabbed the door knob.

"He wouldn't. We'll interview the Duvalls and then we'll go visit Stephanie. See you fellas later."

Valerie hurried after her, and a moment later, Charlene's stretch Impala hit the expressway on the way out to Aurora, Colorado. They found the unassuming cottage where they'd dropped off Tom and Margaret Duvall the day before. Charlene knocked at the door, and Tom answered.

"Oh, hello, Detective. I wasn't expecting to see you here again. What can I do for you?"

"You can call me Charlene," she told him. "My partner and I were just in the area, and we stopped to see how you and Margaret are doing after your ordeal yesterday."

Tom's shoulders sagged. He closed his eyes and compressed his lips.

"We're getting through it, Detective. That's about the best I can say."

Charlene nodded.

"I'm so sorry for your loss. Is there anything we can do?"

Tom squinted at her. A five-o'clock shadow covered his face, and he wore his slippers instead of regular shoes. He must have just gotten out of bed.

"I don't suppose you're any closer to finding out who killed Tim, are you?"

"As a matter of fact," Charlene replied, "that's one of the reasons we came to see you. Do you mind if we come inside and talk to you some more about the shoot-out at the cafe?"

Tom sighed and stepped back from the door.

"I suppose it can't do any harm."

He shuffled into the house, and Charlene and Valerie entered after him. The place reeked of cheap coffee, and used plates and cups sat on the dining table near the entrance. On the other side of the dining room, Margaret Duvall sat on the couch in her bath robe and fluffy pink slippers. At least her hair was combed, but she wasn't wearing any make-up. Bright red rings surrounded her eyes, and when Valerie and Charlene walked in, she blew her nose on a handkerchief.

Tom sat down next to Margaret and took her hand. Charlene looked around. Then she sat down in the chair opposite the couple, and Valerie took another seat on the other side. Tom glanced at his wife.

"As you can see, Detective, we're not doing very well at all."

"I know Tim's death must have been a terrible blow for you," Charlene replied.

"This was the first chance Margaret got to meet my brother," Tom went on. "We'd been looking forward to his visit for months, and this is how it had to end."

Charlene stiffened.

"Why hadn't they met? Tim lived in Salt Lake City. He couldn't have visited anytime."

Tom shrugged.

"He could have, but he didn't."

"Were you two on bad terms or something?" Valerie asked.

"No, no, nothing like that," Tom replied. "Tim was really busy with his work and everything else, and...."

"What everything else could keep him that busy that he couldn't come to Denver to meet his own sister-in-law?" Valerie asked. "Did he have a wife and kids of his own?"

"No, he never married or had kids," Tom replied. "He was just really busy. He never got a free moment to go visiting around the country." He looked down at his wife again, and she burst into loud sobs. She pressed her handkerchief to the underside of her nose and sobbed into it.

Valerie examined the room for something cheery to use to change the subject.

"What about you two? Do you have children?"

"They're grown and gone now," Tom replied.

"Are they in Denver, too?" Valerie asked. "Maybe you could call on them for support in your time of need."

Tom shook his head.

"Our son is married with three children, and lives in Pennsylvania, and our daughter is a doctor in Reno. Neither of them has the time to drop everything and tend to their poor old parents."

"Oh," Valerie muttered. "I'm sorry to hear that."

Charlene cleared her throat.

"Can you tell us anything about your brother's business?"

"He ran an organic food wholesale business," Tom began.

"We know that," Charlene replied. "I'm wondering if you can tell us why he came to Denver. You said at the cafe he came out here for business and he visited you at the same time. Do you know what brought him here?"

Tom cast an anxious look at his wife.

"I couldn't tell you that. I'm sure it was something very mundane like working out a distribution contract or something like that. His life was pretty boring."

"How do you know?" Valerie asked. "If you hadn't seen him in.... how long did you say you and Margaret had been married?"

Tom drew himself up, and for a moment, his pride wiped away his depression.

"We've been married thirty-five years next April."

Valerie gasped.

"Wow! Congratulations!"

Tom closed his eyes and bowed his head.

"Thank you."

Valerie went on.

"So you hadn't seen your brother in thirty-five years, and...."

"I've seen him," Tom interrupted.

"But you said…" Valerie stammered.

Tom shook his head.

"I visited him in Salt Lake City a couple of times. I went there for conferences through my job at the hospital, and I got together with him. He showed me around his business, but that's all. He never had a girlfriend. He never had any hobbies. He never did anything but work."

"But our research shows his business wasn't that big," Valerie pointed out. "He couldn't have been working so hard that he couldn't take time off if he wanted to."

Tom shook his head again.

"All he ever did was work. He cared more for his work than his own family."

How Charlene ever got them out of that cottage, Valerie could never remember, but she was happy to wipe the experience from her memory. The whole interview was a waste of time, and they left it as ignorant about the cause of the murders as when they went in.

She rolled down the Impala's window and let the wind catch her cheeks and hair. All of a sudden, Charlene tugged at her sleeve. Valerie brought her head back inside the car.

"What?"

"I asked you a question," Charlene told her.

"Sorry. I didn't hear it." Valerie adjusted her hair. "What did you say?"

"I'm still not convinced Tim Duvall was killed on purpose," Charlene replied. "I still think his death could have been accidental."

"Even if the shooter at the cafe didn't mean to hit Tim," Valerie pointed out, "it's still capital murder. He killed an innocent bystander in the commission of another violent crime. He's just as guilty as if he walked in there to kill Duvall."

"I know," Charlene replied. "But still, if he didn't mean to kill Tim, we're barking up the wrong tree."

Valerie shook her head.

"I'm more convinced than ever that there's something fishy going on in the house of Duvall. You looked around that house. There wasn't one single picture of their children or grandchildren on the walls. And you can't tell me a man wouldn't take a few weeks off here and there in thirty-five years to drive or fly from Salt Lake City to Denver to meet his brother's wife. Nobody is that busy."

Charlene nodded.

"That's been bothering me, too. They must have had some serious family conflict going on."

"And don't forget Tim's clothes," Valerie went on. "Show me the organic wholesaler who wears an Armani suit. It doesn't make sense. And they want us to believe his life was so boring he didn't even have a girlfriend? Give me a break!"

Charlene cocked her head to one side.

"You're starting to sound like Jeff."

Valerie blushed.

"He's turning out to be quite an investigator."

Charlene shook her head.

"He's grasping at straws. That shows his lack of experience."

Valerie eyed Charlene.

"I thought his theory was a good one. I didn't hear you come up with anything to disprove it. We're investigating a mob war, and one of the principals' sons just got shot in the back. It makes sense his death was related to the war."

Charlene shrugged.

"We still don't have anything to substantiate that, and if I was you, I wouldn't go off half cocked over anything Jeff Everson says."

Valerie shot her partner a critical look.

"Why do you have it in for Jeff? Why can't you at least entertain a decent theory? Tiko thinks the world of Jeff, and he thinks the theory is a good one."

Charlene rolled her eyes.

"Tiko doesn't have two brain cells left to rub together. He spent too many years on the other side to know his right hand from his left."

Valerie turned back to the window.

"You're wrong about Jeff. He's going to be one of the best investigators on the Strikeforce Team. You mark my words."

Chapter 5

Charlene knocked on the door at the Captain's Arms Apartments. A statuesque woman with blonde hair down to her waist answered the door. Except for the tears staining her cheeks, she could have stepped off a high fashion runway. She wore tight jeans around her shapely legs, and a gold chain dangled in the cleavage of her shirt.

"Stephanie Bowen?" Charlene asked.

"Yes?" she replied.

Charlene flashed her badge.

"We're Federal agents investigating Tony Eno's death. Do you mind if we ask you some questions about him?"

Stephanie went back inside without answering, and when the two investigators entered the room, they found her curled up in a velvet armchair with a cat on her lap. She sniffed her tears away. Valerie and Charlene took the couch across the room.

"I guess you heard about Tony," Charlene began.

Stephanie bowed her head and nodded. Tears sprinkled her cat's back, and Stephanie brushed them away.

"I'm very sorry for your loss," Charlene went on. "Is there anything we can do?"

Stephanie shook her head.

"This is the end of my dream to marry Tony. No one can do anything for me. My life is over."

"I'm sure Tony's family will take care of you," Charlene told her. "You were going to marry him. I'm sure they won't leave you out in the cold."

Stephanie shook her head.

"I don't want any hand-outs from them. I just want Tony, and I'll never have him again. I don't know how I can even go on living."

"Now, don't start talking like that," Charlene chided.

"There's always a reason for living, even in the darkest depths of despair. You should concentrate on helping us find out who killed him."

"What can I do?" she asked.

"Do you know anybody who disliked Tony enough to kill him?" Charlene asked.

"I can't think of anybody," Stephanie replied. "Everybody loved him. He was the sweetest, kindest, nicest guy in the world."

"He might have been," Charlene returned. "Either way, somebody wanted him dead. Do you know anything about his employment at the Morning Maven? We hear he got the job through his mother. Is that true?"

"He couldn't have gotten the job if he wasn't qualified for it," Stephanie replied. "His mother never gave him anything he didn't deserve. She only told him the job was open. She didn't help him get it."

"Did he have any experience managing a cafe before he got the job?" Valerie asked. "He's Frank Lukeman's son, so he must have had a privileged life. I don't see how he could have had much experience working in cafes."

"He had a degree in business management from CU," Stephanie told her. "He'd worked in a couple other organizations during his university training. That's how he got his experience. This was his first time working in a cafe, but he was a good manager. He could manage any kind of business with his eyes closed."

"Do you know of a man named Tim Duvall?" Charlene asked. "Do you know if Tony had any dealings with him recently?"

"I don't recognize the name," Stephanie replied. "But Tony didn't tell me every detail of his business. He was a professional, and he kept work matters confidential."

"What about his personal life?" Valerie asked. "We hear he had a lot of friends, but no-one can live without pissing somebody off some time. Did he have a lot of female friends that would make other guys jealous of him? Did he ever get into trouble at clubs when you went out?"

Stephanie shook her head. "I never saw him get into trouble, and men and women all loved him equally. He never played around with other men's girlfriends. He was too good for that."

"No one who winds up shot four times in the back is that good and that loved," Valerie insisted. "There must have been someone who hated him enough to kill him."

"You'll see," Stephanie replied. "When you start to investigate him, you'll find out he was some kind of angel sent down from heaven. Maybe you made a mistake. Maybe whoever killed him did it by accident. Maybe they hit the wrong man." She broke down crying again.

"What jobs did Tony do for Frank Lukeman?" Charlene asked. "Did Frank use the cafe as a front for laundering money or something?"

"Tony didn't work for Frank," Stephanie told them. "He was perfectly clean."

"He couldn't be," Valerie shot back. "He's the son of a major mafioso. It would be unheard of if he didn't wind up working in the family business."

Stephanie's mouth screwed up in silent sobs.

"He was too pure for that. He never wanted to have anything to do with that violence and trouble. He told Frank the same thing when he was twelve years old, and he kept his nose clean his whole life. He didn't work for Frank. He never did."

Charlene sighed.

"I understand why you wouldn't want to cooperate with us, Stephanie, but…."

"I *am* cooperating with you," Stephanie cried.

"I don't know what you want me to say, but everything I've told you is the truth. Tony was clean. You can ask Frank if you don't believe me. Tony took me to meet Frank at his house, and Frank told me the same thing. Frank couldn't believe it himself, but Tony wanted to live a clean life, and he did."

Charlene stood up, but just then, Stephanie's phone rang. She pressed it against her head.

"Hi. Yeah, I heard. Thanks, I appreciate it. I'll see you later. I'm talking to the cops right now." She hung up.

"Who was it?" Valerie asked.

Stephanie looked up into her eyes through a film of tears.

"It was my mother."

"Are you close?" Valerie asked.

Stephanie's chin dropped to her chest and she nodded. Her shoulders shook with silent tears.

Valerie and Charlene left her there with her cat for comfort. The Impala cruised through the shady streets.

"So Tony Eno was a saint from heaven."

Valerie snorted.

"She was in love with him. What did you expect her to say?"

Charlene yanked the wheel to one side and the Impala careened off the expressway. Valerie screeched in surprise.

"Hey, where are you going?"

Charlene nodded at the houses beyond the windshield.

"Frank Lukeman lives here."

Valerie's eyes popped out of her head.

"So? You can't just roll up to his house and question him like any other suspect."

"Why not?" The Impala hopped the curb and Charlene hit the brakes.

"He's a citizen like any other. If he had anything to do with the murders at the cafe, we can question him. He doesn't get special treatment for being a mob boss. Stephanie said we could ask him if Tony was clean and he would tell us, so that's what we're going to do."

Valerie shook her head.

"You can't be serious."

Charlene paid no attention to her, and by the time Valerie had struggled out of the car, Charlene was already up the walk and ringing the bell. A maid in a black and white outfit answered the door.

"We're here to see Frank Lukeman."

The maid arched her eyebrow.

"Do you have an appointment."

"Yeah." Charlene took her badge out of her pocket and held it up in the maid's face. "Here's our appointment."

The maid slammed the door in their faces, and footsteps rang through the big house. Charlene grinned at Valerie.

"I love this job."

A moment later, the footsteps came back and the same maid jerked the door open.

"Mr. Lukeman will see you now."

Charlene beamed at her, and the two investigators followed her inside. She escorted them through a pristine Victorian house and out into the garden behind it. At a table in the gazebo sat a middle-aged man with salt and pepper hair and wire rimmed spectacles sitting on the bridge of his nose.

Valerie stared at him.

"Are you Frank Lukeman?"

He smiled and waved his hand over the tranquil garden surrounding him.

"Whose house did you mean to come to? Sit down. I hear you want to question me about Tony's death."

The investigators sank onto a bench on the opposite side of the gazebo.

"How did you know we came about Tony?"

He tucked his tie down between the lapels of his jacket and straightened his watch on his wrist.

"Why else would you have come? I've been waiting for some law enforcement officer to show up on my doorstep. Now here you are, so ask me whatever you want."

Valerie and Charlene exchanged glances. Valerie spoke up first.

"All right. Why does Tony have a different last name if you're listed on his birth certificate as his father?"

Frank burst out laughing.

"You don't waste any time, do you? Okay, if you want to play hard ball, I'm game. I didn't have anything to do with Tony's name. His parents named him before I ever met his mother."

"Then the rumor is true," Charlene remarked. "Tony has a different father. If that's true, why the changed birth certificate?"

Frank turned toward her.

"Back in those days, people had different ideas about divorce and raising children. People thought that if a woman had children and got a divorce, her new husband ought to adopt the children and the old husband should disappear from the picture. The courts would complete an adoption of the children and completely rewrite their birth certificates with the new husband listed as the father. They would wipe out every record of the child's natural father and then seal the records."

Valerie's mouth fell open.

"How could they do that? Didn't they have any respect for the children's natural father?"

Frank shrugged.

"They did it all the time. That's the way the process worked back then. There was no awareness of the need for children to know their natural fathers or for the fathers to be a part of their children's lives. They did the same thing with Tony. I adopted him and raised him as my own, and he never had anything to do with his natural father."

"Then he really is Danny Seagall's son," Charlene exclaimed. "Did he know?"

Frank shook his head.

"Danny Seagall was not Tony's father. You've been reading too many gossip columns."

"If it wasn't Danny," Valerie asked, "who was it?"

Frank shook his head.

"I can't tell you because I really don't know. You'll have to ask Tony's mother. She's the only one who knows for certain."

"Didn't you see the adoption paperwork before you signed it?" Valerie asked.

Frank smiled.

"You really know your stuff, don't you? I saw the papers, but the name was blacked out. Edith didn't want me to know."

"Then how do you know Danny wasn't the father?" Charlene asked.

"She got pregnant at a commune in Southern California," Frank replied. "Danny Seagall lived his whole life on the East Coast until he moved to Denver. He and Edith were on opposite sides of the country when she got pregnant with Tony. Tony's father was some hippy from LA, not a Jew from Connecticut."

The two investigators looked at each other again. Another question was nagging at Valerie's mind and she couldn't stay quiet any longer.

"You don't seem very sad about Tony's death. If you raised him as your own, shouldn't you be grieving over him?"

Frank cocked his head to one side.

"I suppose that makes you suspect me of killing him. You're Federal agents, so you must have studied up on my record before you came here. You know I've been implicated in dozens of hits on lots of different people. If I killed Tony, I wouldn't hide it from you. I would announce it to the world. I would brag about it. I would tell the world I knocked off Edith and Danny's bastard son."

"You should be more careful about admitting guilt in serious crimes," Valerie told him. "You could be indicted for it."

"You should know better than that, Agent.... what's your name?" he asked.

"Inglewood," she told him. "Valerie Inglewood."

"You should know better than that, Agent Inglewood," he went on. "You should know that one confession does not an indictment make. Even if I gave you a written, signed, notarized affidavit testifying that I shot Tony with my own hands, you would still have to find some solid proof that my confession was valid. It wouldn't stand up in court if you didn't. I could take out an ad in the paper and it wouldn't mean a thing without proof."

Valerie blushed and looked down at her hands.

"That's true."

"I didn't kill Tony, nor did I order anyone else to do it," he told her. "I wouldn't hesitate to tell you if I did."

"Do you know who did?" Charlene asked.

Frank shook his head.

"I have no idea, but if I had to guess, I would say it wasn't a mob hit."

"What makes you say that?" Valerie asked.

"Think about it," Frank told her. "Tony had no mob connections beyond me and his mother. He never worked in any mob-related business. He was universally liked, and he had a lot of good friends. He worked hard at that cafe and he made good money. You'd better wake up pretty early in the morning if you want to find someone with a motive to kill him, but it won't be me, or Danny Seagall, or anybody else related to organized crime."

Charlene leaned forward.

"Do you know anything about his relationship with Stephanie? Do you know if they had any problems?"

"What couple doesn't have problems?" Frank asked. "I'm sure they had the same problems everybody else had. But Stephanie didn't kill him, either. She loved him more than anything. They were going to get married, just as soon as she finished her degree."

Charlene nodded and stood up.

"I think that's all we have for you right now, Mr. Lukeman. We'll be in touch if we need to question you again."

"You know where to find me," he called after her.

Valerie hung back.

"Just one more question."

He smiled.

"Sure thing."

"Did you order that shooter to blast the Morning Maven Cafe?" she asked. "Was that part of your war with Danny Seagall."

"That's two questions," Frank pointed out, "but no, I didn't order it, and I can't think why Danny would order it, either. The Morning Maven wasn't part of our fight. I didn't know anything about the Morning Maven until yesterday except that Tony was the manager. That's all I can tell you."

"Did you know a man named Tim Duvall?" Valerie asked.

"Can you think of any reason the shooter would single him out for death?"

A shadow crossed Frank's face.

"Tim Duvall? I know that name. He was at Taste Supreme, that high-end organic restaurant on Nugget Avenue. He was negotiating organic food supplies with the head chef."

"So he didn't have anything to do with your criminal enterprise, either?" Valerie asked.

Frank waved toward the bench.

"If you want to ask me questions, you might as well sit down and make yourself comfortable."

Valerie smiled in spite of herself.

"This is the last question. I promise. Did Tim Duvall have anything to do with your business or Danny's? Was he connected to the mob in any way?"

"Not that I know of," Frank replied. "As far as I know, he was a perfectly law abiding food distributor."

Chapter 6

Charlene stopped the car in front of a nice house in a middle-income suburb.

"What are we doing here?"

"Edith Skipperingham lives here." Charlene tossed her keys into a compartment on the console.

"You didn't tell me we were stopping by to see her," Valerie remarked.

"I only decided a few minutes ago," Charlene explained.

"Since we've seen all the rest of the grieving families, we might as well stop by and see her, too. I'm sure she won't tell us her beloved Tony was an angel from heaven who didn't have anything to do with his father's business. She'll give us the straight dope."

"I hope so," Valerie muttered. "I hope she can clear up some of the confusion about her son's activities.

Charlene knocked on the door the way she usually did. Valerie didn't even question why Charlene always knocked on the doors. She also always started the questioning, but somehow Valerie always wound up finishing it. Now why was that?

A lady almost as tall as Charlene answered the door. She wore her frosted grey hair coifed in swirls around her head, but her clothes were chic and modern. She could have stepped off the streets of Paris. She surveyed the two investigators up and down. Valerie had never felt so much like a bug under a microscope.

"Edith Skipperingham?"

"You must be the cops investigating Tony's death," Edith replied.

Both investigators sighed.

"We are."

"Then you better come in," Edith told them. "I've been waiting for you."

She stuck them in wicker chairs in her blisteringly warm conservatory, and she stretched out on a divan nearby. She brushed her hand through the fronds of a tree fern while she talked.

"I had a feeling Tony was in danger, but he wouldn't listen to me."

"What made you think he was in danger?" Valerie asked.

"Just a feeling I got," she replied. "Call it intuition. I get these premonitions sometimes when something's about to happen. I can't explain it any better than that."

"It must be because you're Tony's mother," Valerie remarked.

"No, it isn't that," Edith replied. "I get these premonitions about everybody, all the time. This is the first time I've had one about Tony, but I was right as usual."

"Did you have a feeling he would die?" Charlene asked.

"Not that he would die," Edith replied. "Only that something would happen to him. I tried to warn him, but he only laughed and said he couldn't order his life around my feelings."

"That must have made you mad," Valerie remarked.

"Not really," Edith replied. "He was right, actually. You can't drop everything just because your old mother has an intuition. You need something more solid than that if you want to convince people to take action."

"What did you want him to do?" Valerie asked. "Where did you think the danger was coming from?"

"He could have cut some of the negative influences out of his life," Edith replied. "He could have been more careful about the people he kept company with. That was Tony's one true fault. He couldn't discern good people from ones who wanted to use him to their own advantage."

"Stephanie says everybody loved him," Valerie told her. "She says he was good and kind to everybody and had no enemies."

Edith fiddled with her fern fronds.

"He was good and kind to everyone, but everyone wasn't good and kind to him in return. I wish they had been."

"Which of his friends did you know?" Charlene asked. "I'm surprised Tony introduced you to his friends."

"He didn't introduce me to very many of them," Edith admitted. "But when he did, I thought he could have done better. They all wanted something from him. Some of them wanted him to introduce them to Frank. Some of them wanted money. Others wanted him to give them jobs. Almost none of them truly valued him as a person."

"What influence did he have with Frank?" Valerie asked. "Both Frank and Stephanie told us Tony had nothing to do with his father's business, and that he was perfectly law-abiding."

"But his low-life friends either didn't know that or didn't believe it," Edith replied. "They thought it was a cover to keep his mob involvement a secret. The more he told them he wasn't involved in the mob, the more they pressured him to bring them into the business, too. It was a no-win situation, but he never would cut those people adrift. He couldn't stand to lose anybody, no matter how much of a leech they were."

"I guess he introduced you to Stephanie," Valerie remarked. "He brought her to meet Frank. He must have done the same thing with you."

Edith's head whipped around, and the benign superiority vanished from her face. Her voice hissed through her clenched teeth.

"Stephanie was the worst of the bunch. I couldn't stand her."

Valerie stiffened.

"What do you mean? She loved him, and she's devastated by his death. It's a good thing she has her mother to support her or she might be in real danger of hurting herself over this."

Edith stared at her.

"Her mother?"

Valerie nodded.

"She got a call from her mother while we were interviewing her. They're very close."

Edith swallowed hard.

"Her mother's dead. Her mother died when she was ten years old. She told me so herself."

Valerie blinked.

"But why would she lie about it?"

Edith snorted.

"Stephanie Bowen is a lying tramp. She's the worst gold-digger that ever walked the face of the earth. She never liked Tony, and she treated him like trash. Why he stayed with her so long I'll never know. She cheated on him more than once, but he would never believe it."

"How did you find out?" Valerie asked.

"I know the man who owns the bar where she works," Edith replied. "He told me how she would hook up with a new guy every week. More than one person tried to confront Tony about it, but he was too trusting and tender-hearted to believe that she would ever betray him that way."

"But they planned to get married," Valerie pointed out. "Why would she marry him if she wanted to mess around with other men?"

"She was marrying him for his money," Edith replied. "She thought he had access to Frank's money and power, and she wanted that for herself. That's the only reason she stuck with Tony for so long."

Valerie shook her head. How could she take in all this information at once? Nothing made any sense anymore.

"Frank Lukeman wasn't Tony's natural father. There's a rumor going around that Danny Seagall was Tony's father, and..."

Edith burst into loud gales of laughter.

"Danny Seagall! That's a good one!"

Valerie and Charlene smiled, too.

"All right. It's a bizarre story, I grant you. Would you mind telling us who his father was?"

Edith wiped her eyes on her sleeve.

"I'm sorry. I just can't get over it. Danny Seagall!"

"Did you ever have a relationship with Danny?" Charlene asked.

Edith swallowed her laughter.

"I never had any relationship with Danny other than a business relationship. I've never touched any part of Danny's body except his hand to shake it. And Tony's father is Martin Francis Eno of San Diego."

Charlene frowned. "I've never heard of him."

"No one has," Edith replied. "Martin isn't connected to…. well, to anything. He was a freshman at San Diego State when I met him, and he went on to become an accountant. He has a wife who's a PA and three children who are now in high school. He's the most boring, suburban man you can imagine." She giggled to herself. "Danny Seagall! Ha!"

Valerie suppressed a grin.

"All right, Edith. That's all we wanted to talk to about for now. If you think of anything more that might help us with our investigation, you be sure to contact us."

She escorted them out.

"I will."

Charlene got behind the steering wheel, but she didn't start the car.

"What do you think?"

"I think somebody's just given us a big song and dance to make us leap around and make fools of ourselves," Valerie replied. "Someone is lying through their teeth about Tony Eno."

"But who?" Charlene asked.

"And not just about Tony Eno," Valerie went on. "One of these people has a very distorted view of Stephanie Bowen, too. Either she was a sweet, loving soon-to-be wife who doted on Tony and couldn't live without him, or she was a lying, conniving, calculating sleaze. She couldn't be both."

"Edith could be the lying, conniving, calculating one," Charlene pointed out. "She could have been jealous of anybody planning to take away her beloved son. She could be one of those vindictive mothers-in-law who does everything to sabotage her daughter-in-law."

"Do you believe that?" Valerie asked.

"I don't know who or what to believe anymore," Charlene replied. "My mind is bursting."

"I thought Edith was very level-headed," Valerie remarked. "I thought she had a pretty clear grasp of Tony's situation. She tried to warn him about negative influences in his life, but he wouldn't listen. It's a classic story."

"What about all that stuff about her intuitions and her premonitions?" Charlene asked. "She sounds kind of unstable to me."

"Lots of people have premonitions," Valerie replied. "And they usually turn out to be correct. She had a feeling Tony was in danger, and she was right. He thought everybody loved him and no one would do him any harm, but he was wrong, and his mother was right. Mother always knows best."

Charlene chuckled and started the motor.

"I wouldn't mind going back to Frank Lukeman's, now that we've visited Edith, to ask him about her. I bet he has some pretty interesting stories to tell about her. He could give us a heads-up on her kooky ideas."

"Rumor has it they've stayed friends ever since they broke up," Valerie told her.

"I know they've done a few business deals together, and they've been seen together at functions and banquets."

"You should know better than to listen to rumors around this town," Charlene scolded. "If they're such good friends, why did they split up?"

"It actually wasn't a rumor," Valerie replied. "I read an interview with her in the *Herald*."

"The *Herald*!" Charlene guffawed with laughter. "You should never read the *Herald*, and if you do, never repeat anything you read there."

"This was a real interview with Edith Skipperingham," Valerie explained. "She said the only reason she split up with Frank Lukeman was because of the criminal nature of his business. She wanted to get into business herself, and she couldn't get into anything legitimate as long as she was married to him. No one would take her seriously, and no one would trust her with their money. She had to make a clean break from him, even though she never stopped loving and respecting him as a person."

"That just goes to show how mentally unstable she is," Charlene shot back. "She loved and respected a known mafioso, a killer, a drug dealer, a fraudster — shall I go on?"

Valerie turned away.

"You can stop now."

Charlene eased the Impala into a gas station and stopped next to the premium pump.

"Let's stop by the commissary for lunch."

Valerie leaned back in the seat. "Okay. I'm hungry, too."

Charlene went inside to pay, and Valerie drifted with her own thoughts. Their interview with Frank Lukeman raised more questions than it answered. She let her eyes close. She didn't realize she was so tried from staying up deep into the night with Jeff, talking and.... well, not talking.

This was the problem she foresaw living next door to him. They both found it irresistibly easy to sneak into the next room and tumble into bed together whenever they found themselves alone. They would have to get tough on themselves before their work started to suffer from chronic sleep deprivation.

Valerie had started to drift into a doze, when a deafening crash startled her awake. One glance toward the gas station was all she needed to size up the situation in an instant. A masked man stood in front of the cash register pointing a pistol at the clerk. The poor clerk fought to control his shaking hands in a fumbling effort to get the cash register open. Through the open door, Valerie could just make out the customers cowering on the floor behind the gunman. Where was Charlene? She wouldn't be cowering on the floor. She could have shot the gunman in the back with her service pistol and put a stop to this.

But Charlene was nowhere in the station. Then Valerie caught sight of her coming out of the bathroom. She didn't suspect a thing, and when she entered the station, the gunman whirled around and threatened her with his gun. In an instant, Charlene dropped flat on the floor with her arms outstretched like any other helpless bystander.

Valerie jerked her door open and strode across the tarmac toward the open door. The gunman had his shoulder turned toward her, and didn't see her draw her own pistol. He couldn't keep track of the clerk, and the customers, and her, all at the same time.

Once he turned his back on the store, Charlene moved her hands around behind her back and stuck them down into the waistband of her slacks. With any luck, the clerk would have a shotgun or a pistol under the counter. No matter which way the gunman turned, someone would shoot him from behind and the danger would be over.

Valerie got to the door, and as she'd hoped, the gunman saw her out of the corner of his eye. He turned, bringing his gun to bear on her. Charlene pulled her weapon from her holster and pushed herself silently to her feet. At that moment, the gunman fired at Valerie. She covered her head with her arms and ducked into the station. She dove behind the magazine rack, but it didn't offer much shelter. Bullets ripped through the pages and hit the bottles of windshield wiper fluid on the bottom shelf. Soapy liquid flooded the floor.

Valerie slipped in the puddle and went down on one knee. Charlene planted her feet wide and leveled her pistol at the gunman, but he didn't take his eyes off Valerie. In answer to her prayers, the clerk came up from behind the counter with a big pump action shotgun in his hands, all his shaking and fumbling gone. He didn't even bother to aim. He sprayed the whole station with buckshot, but none of it hit the gunman.

In response, the gunman turned on him, just as Charlene fired, and in the act of turning, he moved out of the path of the bullet.

It crashed through the front window and sent a shower of broken glass over Valerie's head. She crouched for cover again and clamped her eyes shut. This couldn't be happening all over again, surely, not after the Morning Maven shoot-out. Could Frank Lukeman be responsible for this shooting, too?

Another smattering of buckshot blasted through the station, and this time, some of it hit the gunman in the neck and arms. He shot at the clerk and grazed the man's ribs. The clerk went down behind the counter and took his shotgun with him.

Charlene and Valerie came up at the same moment and hammered the gunman with shot after shot from their guns. He spun around with his pistol raised, but he wasn't shooting anybody anymore. He teetered and fell, and his gun skidded across the floor and came to rest next to the Slushie dispenser.

Valerie let her gun hang at her side. She glanced over at Charlene.

"Are you all right?"

Charlene nodded and peeked over the counter.

"You can come out now, George. He's finished."

The clerk emerged from behind the counter with his hand pressed to his ribs. Charlene took out her phone.

"I'll call the paramedics."

"I don't need the paramedics," George replied.

"No, but he does." Charlene nodded toward the fallen gunman. "Hey, you don't suppose this has anything to do with the Morning Maven case, do you?"

"Why would it?" Valerie asked. "You saw him. He was trying to rob the station. This didn't have anything to do with the case."

Charlene shrugged.

"We just got finished questioning Frank Lukeman about the murders, and now this happens. It can't be mere coincidence."

"Why can't it?" Valerie asked. "He isn't exactly trying to bump us off to stop us investigating."

Charlene rummaged in the gunman's pockets and took out his wallet.

"Max Frick. That's some handle. I'll put it through the database and see what I can come up with." She twiddled with her phone for a minute. "Nothing. He's a small-time crook with a dozen convictions for shoplifting and petty theft."

"He doesn't exactly fit the description of a hired killer, does he?" Valerie pointed out.

"We'll connect the dots and join him back to the case somehow." Charlene put her phone away. "Here comes the cavalry."

"There are no dots to connect, Charlene," Valerie insisted. "He was robbing the station. He didn't know anything about us. He must have been on the scene with his gun loaded and his mask in his pocket long before we ever pulled into the pump."

Charlene frowned at her. "You don't know what you're talking about, Valerie. This is Frank Lukeman's way of getting us off his case. He's trying to shut us up before we implicate him for the Morning Maven shootings."

Valerie drew a tense breath.

"We're all on edge after the shoot-out at the cafe. I'm as jittery as you are, and now we've just been caught in the crossfire again. But we can't let this cloud our thinking. This was a random stick-up. Frank Lukeman had nothing to do with the Morning Maven shooting. He said so himself. He told us point blank that if he had ordered the hits, he would admit it. He's done a lot worse in the past and gotten away with it. He has no reason to believe he couldn't do the same thing now, and he has nothing to do with this robbery, either."

"You're not starting to believe him, are you?" Charlene asked.

"Why would he lie?" Valerie asked.

"Frank Lukeman is a career criminal," Charlene pointed out. "He has no reason to cooperate with us."

Valerie shook her head.

"I've interviewed a lot of people, and I can't think of one I'm more inclined to believe. He answered our questions with perfect composure. Nothing rattled him. I think he's telling the truth."

Charlene signed the scene over to the local police and she and Valerie went back to the Impala. Charlene slammed her door and fired up the engine.

"I'm disappointed in you, Valerie. I thought you were more circumspect than this. Frank Lukeman dangled a carrot in front of your nose, and you ran after it like a hungry rabbit. Everything he told us was a lie. He ordered the hits on Tony Eno and Tim Duvall."

"Why would he do that?" Valerie asked. "You heard what he said. He raised Tony himself. He treated Tony like his own son."

"Then why isn't he grieving over his death?" Charlene asked. "Why isn't he bursting into tears the way Margaret Duvall is over Tim?"

"Everybody handles grief differently," Valerie replied. "Besides, there's something odd about Margaret Duvall. She never even met Tim until the day of the shoot-out, and she's carrying on like she's lost her firstborn child. If I had to guess, I would say she's not grieving at all. It looks like an act to me."

"An act!" Charlene cried. "What are you talking about?"

"She's pretending to grieve to hide the fact that she's not grieving at all," Valerie explained. "She's pretending to grieve to make Tom feel better."

"But he's grieving, too," Charlene pointed out. "Now that is the picture of a grieving man. That's the way I would expect Tony's adopted father to act."

"That's just the thing," Valerie replied. "Frank adopted Tony. He wasn't Frank's natural child. Maybe that makes a difference."

Charlene shook her head and pulled away from the curb.

"Either way, we've got nothing. I hope Stephanie can give us some idea of who might have wanted to kill Tony. If she can't, we're sunk. We don't have a single lead connecting Tim Duvall and Tony Eno to the Seagall-Lukeman war."

Valerie cocked her head to one side.

"You know, Charlene, maybe we've been going about this thing all wrong."

"What do you mean?" Charlene asked.

"I mean," Valerie replied, "we assumed the murders were mob related. Maybe they weren't mob related at all."

"Of course they're mob related," Charlene shot back. "What else would they be?"

"Maybe someone who hated Tony snuck into the cafe and shot Tony," Valerie replied. "Maybe it didn't have anything to do with the mob war."

"Then how did the killer just so happen to time the murder with the shoot-out?" Charlene asked. "And how do you explain Tim Duvall's death? If the shooter didn't go into the cafe to shoot Tim – or whoever he went there to kill — then why did he do it? If the shoot-out wasn't mob related, then nothing about this case makes sense."

"I know," Valerie murmured. "I'm just saying….."

"What exactly are you saying?" Charlene asked. "Do you really want me to believe someone took a machine gun into the Morning Maven Cafe and shot the place to pieces and killed Tim Duvall and created a perfect cover for a second killer to shoot Tony in the back without it being mob related?"

Valerie turned bright red and looked down at her hands.

"I know it doesn't make a whole lot of sense."

"That's putting it mildly." Charlene hit the turn signal lever. "Do me a favor. Don't float these wild conjectures unless you've got something to back it up."

"All I'm saying," Valerie replied, "is that we don't have anything to connect Tony Eno or Tim Duvall to the mob. Okay, maybe some wacko shot up the cafe, but that doesn't necessarily mean he was connected to the murders."

"I could believe that about Tony, but not about Tim," Charlene replied. "One thing is certain. The shooter killed Tim Duvall, either accidentally or on purpose. I can't think of any reason why anyone would shoot up a cafe if it wasn't mob related."

Valerie fell silent. She couldn't think of any reason for the shoot-out, either. She stared out the window at the city passing by. She shouldn't have opened her big mouth in the first place. But Charlene wasn't finished.

"Now you're really starting to sound like Jeff."

Valerie's head whipped around.

"What's wrong with that?"

"His rookie habits are rubbing off on you," Charlene replied. "You can't just fire off these wild theories based on nothing but hot air."

Valerie bristled.

"If I'm starting to sound like Jeff, I'll be proud."

Charlene pursed her lips.

"You'll learn one of these days that you can't run an investigation that way."

"Can we talk about something else?" Valerie asked.

Charlene stared at her.

"What's the matter with you?"

"I'm not talking about that anymore," Valerie muttered.

Charlene pursed her lips.

"I've never known you to be so sensitive. Don't tell me you two are getting all mushy on each other. I know you worked together at the Mackenzie Lodge, but I hoped you could keep it professional on the team. I would hate to have to report to Colonel Tomlinson that you two were compromising each other's investigative integrity."

Valerie narrowed her eyes at Charlene.

"When has either Jeff or I been anything but strictly professional on the team? When have either of us compromised our investigative integrity?"

Charlene shrugged.

"Just don't let it happen if you know what's good for you?"

"Are you threatening me, Charlene?" Valerie asked.

Charlene stared out the window.

"I'm just saying."

Valerie turned away and didn't say anything until Charlene parked her Impala in the Strikeforce parking garage. She slammed her door extra hard, but when they got to the stairs leading into the building, Charlene stopped.

"Come on up to the commissary. It's lunchtime."

Valerie shook her head.

"I'm going to the office. There's something I want to check while it's fresh in my mind."

"You're not mad about what I said about Jeff, are you?" Charlene asked. "Let it go."

Valerie's eyes blazed.

"I'm mad as hell about what you said and I'm going to my desk right now to prove you wrong. You've done nothing but bad-mouth Jeff's theories from the word go, and now you're doing the same thing to me. You've got some kind of mental block about listening to a perfectly good theory when it comes from a rookie."

"Valerie...." Charlene began.

Valerie cut her off with a chop of her hand.

"Don't bother to explain. There's not one shred of evidence to indicate the two murders were mob-related, and I'm going to prove to you that it wasn't. You go to the commissary and eat your lunch. I'll see you later."

She spun on her heel and raced up the stairs before she said something else she would regret. Charlene stood at the bottom of the stairs and watched her disappear into the office block. Valerie took the stairs two at a time, and when she got to her desk, sweat stood out on her forehead and her cheeks flushed bright red.

She slowed down when she got to the office and spotted Jeff standing alone in front of the window. He glanced over his shoulder when he heard the door open, and he smiled at Valerie.

"How did it go?"

Valerie threw herself into her chair and opened her computer.

"Terrible. I just had a dust-up with Charlene."

"About what?" he asked.

"About you. That's what," she shot back. "I ought to be drummed out of the service for getting mixed up with you."

He cocked his head to the side.

"How did Charlene find out about us?"

"She didn't," Valerie replied.

"So what happened?" he asked.

Valerie caught her breath.

"We went to see Tom and Margaret Duvall. Tim was a perfectly legitimate businessman with no mob connections at all. And after that, we stopped in to see Frank Lukeman, and he confirmed that neither Tim nor Tony Eno had anything to do with the mob war going on. He never ordered a hit on either one of them, and he doesn't think Danny Seagall did, either."

Jeff frowned.

"But that's impossible."

Valerie held up her hand.

"I said the murders must not be mob related like we thought they were, and Charlene said I was starting to sound like you."

Jeff burst into a broad grin.

"Wonderful."

Valerie bent her head over her computer.

"Exactly."

Jeff sat down opposite her.

"So what's the rub? Don't tell me you got mad at Charlene over that."

"She said we better watch ourselves and not get mushy on each other," Valerie told him. "She said she would hate to report to Colonel Tomlinson that we were anything less than strictly professional."

"But we've always been strictly professional," Jeff pointed out.

"That's what I said," Valerie replied. "That's when I got mad. I said I was coming up here to prove her wrong."

Jeff sat back in his chair.

"I see. Well, do you want me to help you?"

Valerie's head shot up.

"Would you? You're not too busy, are you?"

"I'm not busy at all," he replied. "I was just waiting for Tiko to get back. I don't have anything to do until then."

"Where is he?" Valerie asked.

"He went to the doctor," Jeff replied.

"He had to get his eyes checked. And before that, I had to go through a required orientation for the Department of Justice. It was so boring I could hardly keep my eyes open, and when I got back, Tiko was gone. I haven't done one constructive thing on this case since you and Charlene left. I'd be glad to give you a hand."

Valerie sat up straighter.

"Great. Thanks a lot. I really appreciate it. I hate to admit I'm doing this out of spite, but I don't want to see Charlene again until we have some solid information we can give her about where this case is going. If it is mob related, we need to find some lead that confirms it. If it's not mob related, we have to find something to explain why Mr. Pearl-Tie-Tack shot up the cafe in the first place."

Jeff crossed from the window to the desk.

"Where should we start?"

"I'm going over the records for the cafe now," she replied. "You could do some more digging on the victims."

He knelt down in front of her chair and pulled it toward him by. A buzz of excitement rippled through her.

"What are you doing?" she asked.

"I'm helping you," he replied. "You're all tied up in knots. I'm helping you relax so you can concentrate on your work."

She couldn't laugh. Her mouth hung open in burning desire. He grabbed her knees and pulled her the rest of the way toward him.

She still sat on the chair, but her knees went around his hips and his hands slid up the bottoms of her thighs. Her body opened the rest of the way to receive him.

He kissed her once and left her mouth hungry and gasping for more. Then he slid his hands back down to her knees and up, but this time, he slid them up under her skirt to her panties. In an instant, he was inside, and Valerie couldn't hold back a soft mew of surprise and excitement. He wasn't going to do this right here in the office, was he? Anybody might walk in at any moment.

But he showed no signs of stopping, and she couldn't have stopped even if she wanted to. He dragged her panties down and they disappeared somewhere on the floor. He pushed her skirt the rest of the way up around her hips, and there she was, laid bare for his pleasure. He sighed with satisfaction at what he saw, and Valerie laid her head back against the chair. Her eyes closed, and he took her with him into the great beyond.

Chapter 7

Charlene entered the office still chewing her granola bar. Valerie and Jeff sat opposite each other at their desks with their heads bent over their computers. Charlene looked back and forth between them.

"Aren't you going to eat anything, Valerie?"

"I'll eat something just as soon as I tell you what I found out about the cafe shoot-out," she replied.

Charlene's eyebrows went up.

"Did you find something?"

A radiant smile spread over Valerie's face.

"Yes, I did. The Morning Maven Cafe was in the middle of a major labor dispute between the owners and the staff. The staff planned to stage a walk-out to protest the owners holding back tip money from the credit card receipts that should have gone to the staff. Tony Eno was hired to take the place of the previous manager, a man named Chino Leith. The owners found out that Chino supported the staff and was going to testify against the owners in the civil suit. They fired him before he could do any damage."

"So you think this Chino shot up the cafe?" Charlene asked.

"It wouldn't be the first time a dismissed employee went postal on his former employer," Valerie replied. "It's worth looking into. It explains why someone would shoot up the cafe without any connection to the mob war."

"You still haven't proven that the shooter – whoever he was – killed Tim Duvall on purpose," Charlene pointed out. "If this Chino shot up the cafe, then Tim Duvall's murder really was an accident."

"No, it wasn't," Jeff interrupted.

Charlene whirled around.

"What do you mean?"

Jeff gestured toward his computer.

"I had a look at the victims, but I couldn't find anything about them we don't already know. So I pulled up the Coroner's Report. It says Tony was killed by hollow-point bullets from close range."

"That makes sense," Valerie replied. "Whoever shot him would want a small gun that could be easily concealed. A rifle wouldn't make sense."

"That's not all," Jeff added. "Would you believe Tim Duvall was shot with hollow-point bullets at close range, too. The bullets were .357 caliber. Our postal shooter didn't kill Tim Duvall at all. Someone very close to him shot him with a pistol. The postal shooter only gave the killer the perfect cover to kill him in cold blood."

Charlene stared at him. Then she looked at Valerie. Then she looked back at Jeff.

"This is impossible."

Jeff turned his computer to face Charlene.

"Take a look for yourself. It's right there in the Coroner's Report."

Charlene opened her mouth, but no sound came out. Then she swallowed hard. She turned toward Valerie, and Valerie couldn't have recognized her face in a million years.

"I owe you an apology, Valerie. You were right, and I was wrong. I hope you can forgive me and let it go."

Valerie beamed at her.

"Consider it forgotten. Now let's get busy. We've got a lot of work to do to get this case wrapped up before our boy goes postal on somebody else."

"What about the people who killed Tim and Tony?" Jeff replied. "They're still at large somewhere out there, too. How are we going to find them?"

"Our first stop is to interview Stephanie Bowen," Valerie told him. "Edith was right about someone dangerous taking advantage of Tony, so she might be right about Stephanie, too. Stephanie lied to us about her mother. Maybe she cooked up a bunch of crocodile tears to make us thing she was upset about Tony's death when she was the one who killed him. Edith said Stephanie cheated on Tony more than once, and that she stayed with him for his money. If he found out about her and cut her off, she would have had a motive to kill him."

"What about Tim?" Jeff asked. "How are we going to find out who killed him?"

"I think I already know who killed him," Valerie replied. "The question is why."

She grabbed her computer, and she and Charlene headed for the door.

"Hey, wait a minute," Jeff called after them. "You're not leaving me here and keeping all the action to yourselves."

"You better wait for Tiko to come back," Charlene replied. "You can go out with him. You just started. You don't want to jump the gun."

"You bet I want to jump the gun," Jeff shot back. "You're not walking out of here and leaving me standing here with my finger up my nose. I'm going with you."

"You can't," Charlene replied. "You have to go with your own partner."

"My partner isn't here," Jeff told her. "I'm going with you. Don't even think about trying to stop me."

Valerie laid her hand on Charlene's arm.

"Let him come. He found the missing piece of the puzzle. He deserves to help us wrap up this case."

Charlene hesitated.

"All right. Just try not to get underfoot."

Jeff grinned, but he didn't bother to ask when he ever got underfoot.

The three investigators went down to the parking garage, and the Impala sailed out onto the avenue. Jeff punched buttons on his phone in the back seat.

"I'm sending Tiko a text to tell him I'm with you. If he gets back to the office soon, he can pick up Chino for us."

Valerie worked on her computer in the passenger seat.

"Stephanie works at the Raging Bull downtown. She should be there now."

Charlene parked the Impala in front of the Raging Bull. Even at two-thirty in the afternoon, jukebox music bubbled out of the bar and the stale stench of spilled beer and evaporating alcohol perfumed the air.

"What a charming place. I wish I worked here instead of on the elite Strikeforce Team." The sarcasm was heavy in Charlene's voice.

They stepped into the bar. A few drunks lay asleep on their tables, and Stephanie stood behind the bar polishing the glasses. She barely glanced at Valerie and her friends when they walked in.

"What'll you have?"

"We just have a few more questions about Tony's death," Charlene told her. "You don't mind, do you, Stephanie?"

"I'm not going anywhere." Stephanie spoke with a gravelly rolling of her tongue inside her mouth. No matter how much she looked like a supermodel, she talked like a barmaid.

"I'm working here until midnight."

Charlene looked around.

"If this isn't a comfortable place for you to talk, we could find somewhere more private. You don't have to talk to us in public if you don't want to."

Stephanie set down her glass and propped both hands on the bar.

"Whatever it is you want to ask about Tony, you can ask here. I don't have time to go anywhere else."

"Okay," Charlene replied. "You and Tony were in a serious long-term relationship. You're the only person who can tell us who might want him dead."

"I wasn't in a serious relationship with Tony," Stephanie replied. "I used to be, but that's ancient history."

Charlene frowned.

"How ancient is it? How recently did you end your relationship with him?"

Stephanie shrugged.

"I don't know. Some time ago, I guess it was."

"What happened to him being an angel from heaven?" Valerie asked.

Stephanie laughed but didn't answer. She went on polishing the glasses.

"When did you break up with him?" Charlene asked. "Was it a week ago? Or a month ago or a year ago?"

"I didn't break up with him," Stephanie replied. "He broke up with me."

"But when?" Charlene asked.

Stephanie shrugged.

"I don't remember."

Charlene glanced at Valerie.

"Okay, so you split up. Can you tell me why you broke up?"

Stephanie turned her back on them and straightened the whiskey bottles in rows on the wall behind the bar.

"He caught me playing the field. He didn't like it, and he dumped me. Just like that."

"When we visited you at your apartment," Valerie remarked, "you gave us a big sob story about your life being over. You said he was the kindest, sweetest man alive."

Stephanie made a face.

"I must have been in shock."

"How long were you playing the field before he found out?" Valerie asked.

Stephanie whipped around and stared at her. Then she burst out laughing. She laughed a grating laugh that combined chronic alcoholism with chronic smoking. The sound set Valerie's nerves on end.

"I always played the field, even before I met Tony. He got the idea that we were serious. He took me to meet his parents and told them we were going to get married. But I never rolled that way. Life is too short to stick with one man."

"But you never told him that, did you?" Valerie asked. "If you'd told him up front that life was too short to stick with one man, he wouldn't have gotten serious about you in the first place."

Stephanie shrugged again.

"Tony was a chump until the day he died. End of story."

"Either way, he's dead now," Charlene told her. "He was shot in the back. Can you tell us where you were at the time of his death?"

"I was here, working," Stephanie replied. "Not everyone can have a rich mafioso for a father. Some of us have to work for a living."

"If you'd married Tony, you wouldn't have had to work for a living," Valerie pointed out.

Stephanie raised one eyebrow and grinned.

"Not all the money in the world is worth selling myself to a single man."

Just then, an electronic chirp sounded, and Stephanie took out her phone. She held it to her ear.

"Yeah. All right, but not right now. It ain't a good time. Give me two hours. All right." She hung up.

"Who was it?" Valerie asked. "It isn't your dead mother calling you again from beyond the grave, is it?"

Stephanie waved her hand.

"It's my new boyfriend. He's everything Tony ever wanted to be and more."

"Who is he?" Valerie asked.

Stephanie laughed again.

"Wouldn't you like to know?"

"Yes, I would," Valerie replied. "Can you tell us his name?"

"I can, but I won't," Stephanie countered.

Valerie stiffened.

"I wouldn't play games with us if I was you, Stephanie. We'll find out who your new boyfriend is, one way or the other."

Stephanie fixed her with a sharp gaze.

"What are you going to do? You can't torture me to make me tell you who my boyfriend is. You can live and wonder who he is. I won't tell you."

Jeff spoke up.

"We can confiscate your phone. We can check your call record and find out who just called you."

Valerie smiled.

"Your new boyfriend isn't Chino Leith, is he?"

The smug smirk vanished off Stephanie's face.

"I think it's time for you people to leave. We'll be getting the after work crowd soon, and I have work to do."

"We're not leaving," Charlene told her. "We're just getting started."

Stephanie glared at them for a moment. Then she turned on her heel and strode through a side door.

The investigators waited, but she didn't come back. Jeff and Valerie looked at each other.

"You don't think she's...."

Charlene burst into action. She leapt to the door and yanked it open, but there was no one behind it.

"Quick! Get after her before she gets away. Jeff, you get around the building. See if she's ducked out a back entrance. Valerie, you're with me."

Jeff ran out the front, and Valerie and Charlene dove through the door after Stephanie.

"What did she run for? If she'd played it cool, we could never have proven she was guilty."

"She doesn't strike me as the kind to play it cool," Charlene replied. "Look, there she goes."

They ran down a hall through the darkened building. The passage turned at the end, and they caught a flash of blonde hair racing through another door. A blast of sunshine lit the hall. Stephanie was outside. At that moment, a hail of gunfire rattled the concrete wall of the building. Valerie and Charlene instinctively hit the floor.

The door banged open, and Stephanie staggered back inside. Valerie yanked her .44 from its holster and rocketed up onto her feet.

"She's armed, Charlene! She's on her way back inside."

Valerie took a knee stance and aimed at Stephanie, but not before Stephanie popped off a couple of rounds from her own pistol.

Charlene bounced to her feet and leveled her weapon at Stephanie. Between the two of them, Valerie and Charlene drove her back toward the door.

But when Stephanie tried to escape, another barrage of bullets peppered the wall and the door. Jeff had her pinned down from outside, and she had nowhere left to turn. She raised her arms to protect her head, and her pistol dangled uselessly from her fingers. Valerie fired a few more times, and Stephanie dropped to the floor with her head buried under her arms.

The door banged shut again, and Jeff ceased his fire. Valerie motioned to Charlene, and silence enveloped the building. Valerie stepped forward and tore the gun out of Stephanie's hand. She gave it a glance. ".357 Magnum. I'll bet it's loaded with hollow points, and I'm sure we'll match it to the bullets taken from Tony Eno."

Charlene fished the phone out of Stephanie's pocket and scrolled through the phone log.

"Last call from Chino Baby. So you two planned this whole thing, didn't you? He was going to get revenge on his previous employer, and you were going to pay Tony back for dumping you and robbing you of your marital fortune. It all makes sense." She snapped her handcuffs on Stephanie.

Stephanie struggled and managed to roll over on her back with her hands tucked under her. She spat and cursed.

"That jerk was going to make me the richest woman in Denver. I would have had my cake and eaten it too, if he hadn't walked in on me and Chino *in flagrante delicto*."

Valerie stared down at her.

"That's an awfully big word for a simple barmaid. Where did you learn that?"

Stephanie spluttered some unintelligible gibberish, and Charlene turned toward Valerie.

"This still doesn't explain who killed Tim."

Valerie holstered her weapon.

"Let Jeff take Stephanie in the Impala. Tiko should be back at the office by now. He can show Jeff how to book Stephanie into the county jail until her arraignment hearing. You and I can take a trip out to Aurora to pay a visit to Margaret Duvall."

Chapter 8

Charlene parked the spotless Lexus in front of the Duvall's cottage.

"Are you sure about this?"

Valerie nodded.

"It's the only explanation that makes sense. If I'm wrong, I'll eat my hat."

Margaret answered their knock, and this time, she wore a freshly ironed business suit. Bright red lipstick adorned her mouth, and black eyebrow pencil set off her sparkling brown eyes. Not a trace of red marred her eyes. Only a hint of doubt crossed her face when she spotted the investigators on her doorstep.

"What brings you back out to Aurora?"

"We just have a few more questions about Tim's death," Valerie replied. "Would you mind if we come in?"

Margaret hesitated.

"I'm just going out. Can't it wait?"

"This won't take long," Valerie replied. "And it's very important. We think we've figured out who killed Tim."

Margaret walked back inside, and Valerie and Charlene followed her. Margaret busied herself arranging flowers in a vase while they talked.

"That's good. I would hate to think a maniac was running around loose on the streets. He might attack again at anytime."

"The shooter who destroyed the cafe didn't kill Tim," Valerie told her. "We caught him, and he didn't know anything about Tim."

Margaret spun around.

"But I thought this shoot-out was part of the mob war we keep hearing about. I thought one of those big mob bosses ordered that maniac to destroy the cafe."

"That's what we thought," Valerie replied. "But none of the victims had any connection to the mob, and neither did the cafe. Both victims were killed at close range with pistols. The man who destroyed the cafe didn't kill Tim."

Margaret shook her head and went back to her flowers.

"I'm afraid you detectives have it all wrong. No one killed Tim with any pistol. Everyone in that cafe was flat on their faces at the time. No one could see a thing."

"All the more reason why the killer would have taken that opportunity to shoot him," Valerie pointed out. "There would be no witnesses, and the noise of the shooters' machine gun would drown out the noise of the pistol that killed Tim."

Margaret clucked her tongue and didn't answer. She didn't turn around again. She fussed with her flowers.

Valerie took a deep breath. "Tom said you never met Tim Duvall until the day he died. He said you met him for the first time on this visit to Denver. But that's not true, is it? You knew him before you met Tom, and you kept your relationship a secret. Isn't that true?"

Margaret whipped around, and her mouth hung open.

"What are you talking about?"

"You knew him," Valerie insisted. "You must have had pretty strong feelings for him because you planned to kill him on this visit. I'm guessing you didn't know how you were going to do it, but you took your pistol along just in case you saw your chance. Then, when the shooter attacked the cafe, you pulled your gun and shot Tim in the confusion. No one saw or heard a thing, and everybody assumed the shooter had hit Tim. How am I doing so far?"

Margaret humphed and turned back to her flowers.

"I don't know what you're talking about."

Valerie glanced at Charlene, and Charlene raised her eyebrows.

Valerie sighed and stepped forward. She came to Margaret's side.

"Listen, Margaret. I understand that you don't want to talk to us, but Tim was killed at close range by hollow point bullets. The shooter didn't kill him. You did. If you don't talk to us, we'll get a search warrant, and we'll find the gun you used to kill him. I'm guessing we'll find some other evidence that you had a relationship with him before you married Tom. Am I right?"

Margaret stared at her. She tried to set her mouth in a firm line, but at the last moment, she broke into tears all over again.

"You don't understand. That scumbag broke my heart once, and I couldn't let him do it again. He was coming back here to rub his success in my face. He wore that stupid suit to impress me. Can you believe that?"

Valerie waited in silence and Margaret continued.

"After he left Denver, he was going back to Salt Lake City to get married to some floozy he'd met at a school picnic. I couldn't let him get away with it. If I couldn't have him, then by God, no one else was going to have him either."

Valerie nodded.

"Did he know that you'd married his brother?"

Margaret pressed her handkerchief to her nose and shook her head. Her tears dissolved her eyebrow pencil.

"Neither of them knew anything about each other. I'd kept the secret all these years, and that idiot didn't even recognize me when he shook my hand. That was the final insult. I wasn't sure I was going to kill him until that happened. I know I'm older, but I can't be that worn out that the man I loved most in all the world wouldn't even recognize me. It just goes to show how besotted he was with his new trophy wife."

Valerie put her hand on Margaret's shoulder.

"We'll have to search your house anyway to find the gun. You could save us a lot of trouble if you just tell us where it is."

Margaret sniffed.

"It's in my husband's gun safe. It's registered under his name. I stole it when we went to the cafe to meet Tim. He never even knew it was gone."

Valerie took Margaret by the elbow.

"You'd better come with us. Do you need to call your husband to tell him what's going on?"

Margaret dabbed her eyes and shook her head.

"I'll call him later. Let him think I'm alright a little while longer."

Back at the Strikeforce office building, Valerie tapped her paperwork into a neat square and set it in a folder.

"Three suspects put away. Not a bad haul for a day's work."

Charlene stood up.

"You're right, and I think you deserve a day off after all the work you've put into this case."

Valerie looked up.

"I don't need a day off. I'm happy."

Charlene shook her head.

"I owe you a big apology, Valerie. You were right about this case, and I should know by now to listen to you, no matter how crazy your theories are. And I owe you an apology, too, Jeff. I just wasn't willing to listen to a rookie who'd just come onto the job. We never would have caught any of these suspects if it wasn't for you, and the way you pinned Stephanie down at the Raging Bull was the work of an expert. I couldn't ask for better."

Jeff swelled with pride.

"Thank you, Charlene. This job means a lot to me. I'll do my best to live up to your standards."

Charlene settled down in her chair.

"As soon as Tiko gets back from the county lock-up, we'll go see the Colonel. He has another assignment waiting for us."

Jeff stood up.

"I'm sorry, Charlene, but Colonel Tomlinson will have to wait."

Her head shot up.

"What for?"

Jeff took Valerie by the hand and raised her from her seat.

"I'm taking Valerie out to lunch. We can meet with the Colonel after we get back."

Charlene opened her mouth. Then she broke into a grin.

"All right. You two go have lunch together. You've earned it. I'll see you when you get back."

Valerie followed Jeff down the hall in a dream. She only shook herself out of her reverie when they got to the stair well.

"What are you up to?"

Jeff smiled at her and pulled her closer.

"Just what I said. I'm taking you out to lunch to celebrate our success. Even Charlene says we deserve it."

Valerie glanced back toward the office and shook her head.

"She sure changed her tune. I never would have believed it."

Jeff popped open the stairwell door.

"You did it. You changed her mind about us by proving that your theory was the correct one. Any rational person would have to admit that they were wrong. I'm glad she wasn't too stubborn to see reason."

"You really stuck it to her by saying you were skipping the Colonel's meeting to take me out to lunch." She paused. "You are really taking me out to lunch, aren't you? You weren't just saying that, were you?"

He drew her out into the stairwell, and the door slammed behind them.

"I *am* taking you out to lunch. There's just one thing we need to do first."

She studied his face, but he didn't give her a chance to ask what the one thing was.

He pushed her back against the cold concrete wall, and his weight against her electrified her every nerve. His mouth devoured her lips and his tongue lapped the sweet nectar of her saliva.

His fingers entwined in her hair and pulled her head back to receive his kiss.

Valerie succumbed to his overwhelming presence, and the cells of her body melted into a hot syrup.

Jeff's crushing weight pinned her against the wall, and her being opened to the heavy elixir of passionate desire.

<u>The End.</u>

Don't miss Valerie's next case, in "Bad Intent" – you'll find a taste of that book just after the 'About the Author' section!

About the Author

T.K. Wilde is a long term writer, who writes both fiction and non-fiction, under a number of pen names.

A particular fondness for mysteries, action, and non-standard female characters resulted in this series – we hope you enjoy it!

Books in the Valerie Inglewood Series

The series, in reading order, is

1. Bad Moon Rising

2. One Bad Apple

3. Bad Blood

4. Bad Intent

5. From Bad to Worse

Here is your preview of Book 4 in the series

STRIKEFORCE AGENT

VALERIE INGLEWOOD

BAD INTENT

T.K. WILDE

Chapter 1

Colonel Tomlinson stood behind his desk. He wore plain green army fatigues and lace-up black boots, and he struck quite a contrast to Valerie and Charlene with their pressed business suits and manicured nails. But he stood ramrod erect, and his muscled shoulders strained against his cotton shirt. He could beat any member of the Strikeforce Team on the obstacle course, the shooting range, in the sparring ring, or on a written test.

He held up a case file.

"This is gonna be a tough one, even for you two. I would assign Jeff and Tiko to work with you again, since you did so well together last time. But they're not back from Florida yet, so we're bringing in another expert to help you out."

"Who is it?" Valerie asked.

"He's a law enforcement officer from another high-level investigation unit," Colonel Tomlinson replied. "They're stationed in Arizona, so they work mostly on cross-border cases. But they're even more prestigious and elite than we are. As a matter of fact, they're so hush-hush, you've probably never heard of them."

Valerie and Charlene exchanged glances.

"I'm sure I've heard of them," Charlene remarked. "I've been in this business long enough to know just about everybody from the top down."

"Not even you know about these guys," the Colonel told her. "These guys don't work with anybody. They keep their activities strictly confidential."

"Then why are they working with us now?" Valerie asked.

"One of their suspects escaped," Colonel Tomlinson replied. "They caught him in Laredo and were transporting him back across the border to San Antonio when he escaped again. He made it as far north as Flagstaff, but he was murdered in his room at the Lamplighter Motel before our friends could catch him. Now this expert is investigating his death, and you two are going to help him. Or, I should say, he's going to be helping you. We've been officially assigned the case, but because of the nature of the incident, we're working together on this."

Valerie's eyebrows went up.

"It's a little out of order, isn't it? We've never worked with any other agency before, and if these guys are that elite and that confidential, they won't take kindly to sharing their territory with us. If they already had this guy in custody and let him get away, they'll be on edge about it happening again."

"They won't be on edge about it happening again, because he's dead," Colonel Tomlinson replied.

"But they might be on edge about you making a mess of their investigation. I admit it's a recipe for disaster, and I wouldn't agree to it under normal circumstances. The only reason I am agreeing to it is because they've specially requested this. It seems word of your exploits has traveled through the agencies of this great land. They want your help."

Charlene jerked her head at Valerie.

"It's Valerie's exploits that have traveled, not mine. I've been on the Strikeforce Team long enough, and they never specially requested me. They must want to see Valerie in action."

Colonel Tomlinson grinned.

"Something like that."

Valerie eyed the file in his hand.

"I guess one murder is very like another. We'll work our mojo and solve it, and everyone will be suitably impressed. I only have one question."

"Shoot," the Colonel replied.

"What's the name of this elite investigation unit?" she asked.

"The feds call 'em XQT06," Colonel Tomlinson replied. "But they call themselves the O-Line."

"The O-Line?" Valerie repeated. "That's football slang for the Offensive Line. Why do they call themselves that?"

"They consider themselves the first line of attack in the war across the border," Colonel Tomlinson replied.

"They view the tide of illegals coming across the border as an invasion force, and they see themselves as the front line battalion tasked with repelling that attack."

"Wouldn't that make them the Defensive Line?" Valerie asked.

Colonel Tomlinson shrugged.

"I didn't make up the name. Maybe you can ask your expert yourself. He's coming in to meet you and brief you on the case."

"When?" Charlene asked.

A bell sounded on a tablet computer sitting on Colonel Tomlinson's desk. He bent over it and touched the screen.

"He's here now."

At that moment, the door opened, and a clean-cut man in an immaculate suit strolled into the office. Valerie froze.

"This is Captain Dan Henderson," Colonel Tomlinson told them. "I believe you know each other."

Dan walked right up to Valerie, took her by the hand, and kissed her on the cheek. "We know each other."

Valerie turned bright red, but she couldn't stop smiling at him. For some reason, she didn't take her hand out of his grasp. He gazed down into her eyes with a big grin on his face.

"It's good to see you again, Valerie. I didn't think I would see you again so soon."

Valerie's cheeks burned.

"So you're the one who specially requested that we work on this case."

"I didn't request you because I wanted to see you again," Dan replied. "I wanted to see you again, but I wouldn't use this case to give myself an excuse to track you down. I could have done that anytime. We've had a devil of a time with this case. I was impressed with the way you cracked that EdenCloud case, so I thought we couldn't do any better than to get your help on this."

Valerie dropped her eyes.

"I didn't do anything special at EdenCloud, or on any other case. I've always had help from..... from everybody."

Charlene stepped forward and extended her hand.

"It's good to see you again, Dan. I trust you're putting your father's death behind you. You must be if you're working on cases like this."

Dan shook hands with Charlene, but he didn't kiss her on the cheek.

"Yes, I'm back at work, now that my father is resting peacefully in our family burial plot in Phoenix. My family owes you and Valerie a huge debt of gratitude for the work you did to bring his killer to justice."

Valerie dropped her voice to a murmur.

"Maybe you haven't heard. AngelPie is in a care home for mentally ill teenagers in Missouri. I wouldn't exactly call what happened to her bringing a killer to justice. She's as much a victim of EdenCloud as your father was."

"That's exactly what I mean," Dan returned. "I heard what happened to her. I've followed every single one of those people since the retreat center broke up. What happened to AngelPie was the closest thing to justice we could ever hope for. She's getting the treatment she needs, and all the other crooked members of that loopy outfit are getting what they deserve, too. I heard her mother got audited by the IRS and lost every dime she had."

Valerie suppressed a snicker.

"I heard that, too."

Colonel Tomlinson cleared his throat.

"Well, if you people are finished catching up on old times, perhaps you could take a walk into the briefing room and get started on the present. The body ain't gettin' any colder, if you know what I mean."

Dan bit back a smile.

"Yes, Sir. If you don't mind, Sir, we'll take the case file with us."

Colonel Tomlinson handed him the file.

"By all means. I was just about to give it to Charlene when you showed up. If you need anything else, don't hesitate to let me know."

"Thank you, Sir." Dan did everything short of saluting before he, Valerie and Charlene left the office.

Outside, Charlene gestured toward a room two doors down the hall.

"This is the briefing room. You can give us the details in here."

The three investigators took their places around the table in the middle of the room. Dan opened the case file and laid a big black and white mug shot in front of Valerie and Charlene.

"This is our victim. His name was Crockett Schneider. He was the mastermind behind the biggest illegal immigrant trafficking ring in the Four Corners area. And now he's dead. He was stabbed in the chest and the murder weapon severed his aorta."

Charlene made a sour face.

"Lovely."

Valerie frowned.

"Crockett Schneider? But Colonel Tomlinson said the victim was illegal. That name...."

Charlene interrupted her.

"The Colonel didn't say he was illegal. He said the O-Line worked to curb illegals crossing the border. He never said anything about the victim."

Dan smiled and nodded.

"I knew you two would be onto this case like a pair of rabid pit bulls. Schneider wasn't illegal. He was true blue American."

"Then what was he doing running illegals across the border?" Valerie asked.

Dan snorted.

"He did it for the money, plain and simple. He charged them incredible amounts to smuggle them into the States. When he got caught, he would play dumb and babble away in Spanish, and everyone assumed he was illegal, too. He got deported back to Mexico a dozen times, but that was just his fancy way of getting off the hook so he could turn around and do it all over again. He must have pulled that trick twenty times."

"Clever," Charlene exclaimed.

"If he did it so many times," Valerie asked, "didn't your team know better? Why didn't they keep him here?"

"That's the problem," Dan replied.

"Our team knew about him and his little game, but it wasn't always us that arrested him. We put the word out to as many other agencies as we could not to deport him, but the information didn't always filter through. More than once, the arresting officers didn't even bother to check this mug shot against the characters they found in the back of the truck. They heard a bunch of Spanish and deported everyone with no questions asked. It happens all the time. The most wanted outlaws on our list can get off scot free by pretending to be illegals who don't speak English." Dan's expression was grim, and the frustration he felt about the situation was very obvious.

"Is that what happened this time?" Valerie asked.

"Did he escape from a deportation transport?"

"This time was different," Dan replied.

"This time, two of our team arrested Schneider with a truckload of illegals crossing the border near Laredo. They knew what they had, and they weren't taking him back to Mexico—no way! They were taking him to San Antonio where they had a grand jury all lined up. They were going to roll into town and have Schneider put away within hours."

Charlene waved both hands back and forth.

"Now just hold on there, Cochise. This doesn't make sense at all. The Colonel said he was killed in Flagstaff. You're telling me he was being transported from Laredo to San Antonio. Flagstaff is nowhere near that route. He would have had to travel all the way across West Texas, and then across New Mexico, and then across half of Arizona to get to Flagstaff. That makes no sense."

Dan laughed out loud.

"This is what I love about working with you two. Nothing gets past you."

"So are you telling us he got all the way across the American Southwest before he was murdered?" Valerie asked.

"That's exactly what I'm telling you," Dan replied. "But he didn't run there on foot. He drove there in a car that was waiting for him near Dilley. The O-Liners who arrested him stopped at a roadside gas station to fuel up, and when one of the agents lifted the hood to check the oil and water, Schneider made a break for it. He ran to a car parked nearby. He pulled the keys out of his pocket, turned the ignition, and drove away."

Valerie and Charlene stared at him.

"Just like that?"

"Just like that," Dan replied.

"Did the agents give chase?" Valerie asked.

"They started to," Dan told her. "But they hadn't filled up their gas tank. They didn't make it more than thirty miles before they ran out of the gas, and Schneider rode off into the sunset."

"He rode off into the sunset to Flagstaff, where he was murdered," Charlene added.

Dan laughed. "Do you want to know the weirdest thing?"

"Do you mean weirder than him having the key to the car in his pocket when he was in Federal custody?" Valerie asked. "Or weirder than the car waiting at a place neither he nor anyone else could have known the agents were going to stop?"

"Weirder than that," Dan replied.

"Let's hear it," Charlene told him.

"The weirdest thing," Dan replied, "is that all our evidence suggests he knew he was going to be murdered in Flagstaff."

Valerie frowned. "How do you figure? Why would he go there if he knew?"

Dan opened the file and took out several sheets of paper.

"Take a look. We tracked several members of his organization, and we found out one of his most trusted lieutenants, a certain Emilio Donnelly, turned traitor and switched to a rival organization about three months ago. He joined The Machos."

"The Machos," Charlene repeated. "That's the most dangerous gang operating across the border."

Valerie nodded.

"Not only that, but they've sworn to kill any Gringos they catch transporting illegals into the country. They believe Gringos can't be trusted and they're all working for the Federales."

"But Donnelly is a Gringo name," Charlene pointed out. "Why would a Gringo join an anti-Gringo gang?"

"He's half Gringo and half Mexican," Dan replied. "He contacted The Machos three months ago behind Schneider's back. If he joined, he would have to prove himself by killing Schneider."

"But Schneider must have known Donnelly would come after him and try to kill him," Valerie pointed out. "You can't tell me you found out Donnelly contacted The Machos but Schneider didn't know."

Dan nodded.

"That's what I'm trying to tell you. We intercepted a message, which was sent to one of Schneider's contacts in Juarez, telling him to meet Donnelly at a motel in Flagstaff. In fact, Schneider's getaway car was listed with a rental company in San Antonio under the name Mark Everest, which is one of Donnelly's known aliases. Donnelly arranged the getaway car for him, and Schneider planned to meet him at the motel to pay him for his service or something like that."

Charlene puffed out her cheeks. "Crikey! That's a lot to swallow in one mouthful."

"You're telling me," Valerie exclaimed.

Dan stood up and closed the file.

"You two are coming with me to Texas."

"What's there?" Valerie asked. "Donnelly will be long gone."

"He's in custody in San Antonio right now," Dan replied. "Our team busted one of his illegal trafficking compounds near Sedona. We're going to interview him first before someone decides to rid the world of his pesky ways. After that, we'll go to Flagstaff to check out the motel where Schneider was killed."

Valerie followed him to the door.

"This is going to be an expensive case. First, we have to drive from Denver to San Antonio, then back to Flagstaff, then who knows where."

"We're not driving," Dan told her. "We're flying."

Valerie stopped in her tracks.

"Flying?"

"Yeah, flying," he replied. "You know, in a plane."

She stared at him.

"Plane?"

Dan laughed out loud.

"The O-Line has a plane waiting at the airport. That's how I got here from Phoenix. I didn't drive here in my beat-up old Toyota Corolla."

"What Corolla?" Valerie asked. "You rolled up to EdenCloud in a Cadillac with leather seats. You never drove any Corolla. Who are you trying to kid?"

Dan smiled down at her. A flush of happiness colored his cheeks.

"That was a rental, but you're right. I don't drive a Corolla."

"What do you drive?" Valerie asked.

He dropped his voice to a whisper.

"I drive a vintage Landcruiser."

Valerie snorted.

"I should have known."

"But I have another Cadillac rented while I'm in Denver. Come down to the parking garage with me. I'll give you a ride to the airport."

"Hang on a minute." Valerie ducked into her office and grabbed a blue shoulder bag from under her desk.

Dan raised his eyebrows.

"What's that—your make-up case?"

Valerie slapped him on the arm.

"No, fool. It's my overnight bag for when random Federal agents blow in and want to whisk me across the country with no notice whatsoever. It's got an extra toothbrush and toothpaste, a hair brush, nail clippers, a clean pair of underwear, that sort of thing."

Dan raised his eyebrows.

"You carry underwear around with you on murder cases?"

Charlene stuck her head between them.

"Are you two finished? Can we get going now?"

Valerie turned bright red and walked away. Dan and Charlene followed. Over her shoulder, Valerie overheard them talking.

"I never met an agent like Valerie before. She's full of surprises."

"You don't know the half of it," Charlene shot back. "Do you know what she did the other day? She told Jeff Everson...."

"Who's Jeff Everson?" Dan asked.

Valerie whirled around.

"Do you mind? I thought we were on our way to the airport."

Dan's eyes widened.

"We're just making small talk. There's nothing more to say about the case until we get to San Antonio."

Valerie turned away. She stormed into the stairwell and ran down the steps two at a time, all the way to the parking garage. She couldn't stand around and listen to anything Charlene told Dan about Jeff Everson. Leave it to Charlene to blow the lid clean off that can of worms.

Find out what happens next-

Make sure to get your copy as soon as its released !

Other Books from Dreamstone Publishing

Dreamstone publishes books in a wide variety of categories – here are some of our other bestselling non fiction books:-

Moving Beyond the Unspoken Grief:
A doctor's memoir of her own IVF
journey as a patient
By Dr Sarah Lnyy

Should I Quit?
Resilience for a turbulent world
By Mike Gordon

"Icebreakers : How to Empower,
Motivate and Inspire Your Team,
Through Step-by-Step Activities That
Boost Confidence, Resilience and
Create Happier Individuals"
By Di McMath

All Books available from all Amazon sites and other book stores, and available for Kindle too!

And here are some of our bestselling romance books from Arietta Richmond.

Be first to know when our next books are coming out – sign up for our newsletter at

http://www.dreamstonepublishing.com